A Time of Green

Eleanor Watkins

instant
apostle

First published in Great Britain in 2019

Instant Apostle
The Barn
1 Watford House Lane
Watford
Herts
WD17 1BJ

British Library Cataloguing-in-Publication Data

A catalogue record for this book is available from the British Library.

This book and all other Instant Apostle books are available from Instant Apostle:

Website: www.instantapostle.com

E-mail: info@instantapostle.com

ISBN 978-1-912726-13-4

Printed in Great Britain.

Chapter One
Juniper

My great-grandmother is a remarkable woman. Everyone says so: her daughter (who is my grandmother), Gramps (who is my grandfather and her son-in-law), Dad (who is her grandson), Mom and all her friends and everyone else who knows her. So it must be true.

Of course, I think she's remarkable too. She is almost ninety, and still lives on her own, with just a helper popping in to do the things she can't do any more, like scrubbing the bathtub and changing bed linen and hoovering. She still cooks and dusts and tends to her plants, of which she has a lot, indoors and out, on her porch and in her yard. In fact, she has so many that her yard is a bit jungly, but that's the way she likes it, and so do I. A Mexican father and son, Luis and Mateo, come in on Tuesdays to cut the grass and tidy the shrubs, but she does everything else herself, even the watering, which of course is strictly rationed.

Great-grandmother's name is June, so I call her Nana June, or mostly just Nana. I am named after her, kind of. My name is Juniper, which Nana says is something she's never heard of as a name, and is a plant really, and trust the Americans to think of something like that! She is sometimes a teeny bit scathing of

Americans, which we don't mind despite us being American, because we know she loves us all and has 'embraced the American way of life', as Gran says. Up to a point, that is. Nana must be the only woman in the USA to hang out her laundry on a line. The only one in our neighbourhood, anyway.

'Such a waste!' she tut-tutted to me one day as I held the peg bag for her and passed the pegs. Hanging out her laundry takes a long time, because Nana's fingers are a little arthritic and not as nimble as they used to be. But she insists on doing it herself. 'Clothes should be hung by the hems or waistbands,' she insists, 'otherwise there'll be lumps and bumps to iron out. I can do it. Just pass the pegs.'

I once ventured to say, 'But Nana, why don't you just use the drier like everyone else?'

She'd glared at me then. 'That makes me so cross! Here we are, beautiful hot sunshine and often a little breeze, by the time you hang out a line of washing the first ones are dry already, and yet everyone uses driers! What a waste! And all those KFCs going into the atmosphere!'

'I think it's CFCs, Nana.'

'Well, whatever! Wasteful, with all this ours for free, and we don't make use of it but instead do our best to spoil it…' She gestured at the blue sky, the burning sun, the hummingbirds in the magnolia bush, the blue jay swooping down on the cropped grass to see what it could find.

My mom and dad both work long hours and I knew they'd never have time or patience for hanging out laundry or ironing. They just take things from the drier, fold them and put them away. But I held my tongue.

Nana glanced at me and seemed sorry she'd been cross. 'You're a good girl, Juni. But it's not the way I was brought up.'

Nana becomes very British, and sometimes very border Welsh, when she thinks of her younger days. We would never say 'brought up', we'd say 'raised'. I suppose it amounts to the same thing. She finished pegging out the last towel and made for the patio, sinking into the cushions of the comfy cane chair with relief. She looked at the line of laundry with satisfaction.

'We did the washing on a Monday, always. It took almost all day, so no time for cooking, always cold meat for dinner and bubble-and-squeak from Sunday's vegetables. The boiler would be lit to heat the water, and the wash house would be full of steam. We had to scrub the dirty bits, like collars and cuffs, extra hard. Then they'd go through the wringer.'

I thought of our gleaming Maytag washer and drier where you just threw everything in and pushed buttons. But I love hearing Nana's stories of what she has done in her life, which amounts to a lot of things, including doing a sky-dive for charity in her fifties, paddling down the Colorado river at the bottom of the Grand Canyon in a canoe, camping out in a forest cabin where you had to hang your food high and away from camp because of bears. She's crossed and recrossed the Atlantic several times, visiting family and people she knew back in the UK. I've never got to fly anywhere, except a hop to San Francisco that only took an hour and didn't really count. Mom and Dad always mean to take me to the UK one of these times, but they haven't yet, mainly because they don't get much holiday time and it's hard to get time off together.

Nana took off her sunhat and fanned her face with it. The porch fan whirred but the air seemed just as warm when it was moving. Across the yard a squirrel sprawled on a branch of the orange tree, all four limbs dangling down, just too hot to move. I'm not usually visiting on a Saturday afternoon but my riding lesson had been cancelled.

'Shall I get you a cool drink, Nana?' I offered. She smiled. 'That would be lovely. Get one for yourself too.'

I poured two glasses of pineapple juice from the fridge and put ice in. Nana was dozing when I got back but opened her eyes when she heard the ice clink. Her hearing is remarkable. She smiled and took a long drink. 'Aah, that's good! One thing I do appreciate is a long cold drink on a hot day.'

The porch thermometer registered ninety and rising and the clock said 3.15. Dad was working overtime and Mom had gone to the gym. I was to be home by five. Nana had finished her drink and closed her eyes again. Her tabby cat, Megan, came and rubbed round my legs. I picked her up and tried to cuddle her but she didn't want to stay.

'You have to let cats come to you,' I remembered being told. Megan didn't want to come, she wandered off and lay across the yard under the oleander. I closed my eyes and dozed a little myself. Nothing else to do really. I felt warm and sticky under my shorts and T-shirt and half-wished I'd gone swimming with one of my friends instead of deciding to visit Nana. But she seemed to like having me. I'd take in the laundry for Nana before I left …

I opened my eyes with a start to find Nana looking at me from under the brim of her hat. 'I – I wasn't asleep, not really,' I said.

She smiled. 'Neither was I. It's nice to give your eyes a rest now and then, isn't it?'

I saw it was still only 4 o'clock. It would not begin to cool off for a while yet. And then the mozzies would be out and the cicadas would be chirping their evening song. I liked the cicadas but not the mozzies.

Nana sighed. 'I do miss home sometimes. Especially the spring and summer. There was never heat like this. You'd get sunny days, cloudy days, breezy ones, rainy, drizzly, foggy ones. Hardly ever two the same.'

I couldn't imagine that. Summer here, every day is the same. Blue skies, sun shining down, heat, air con, mosquitoes, cicadas.

Nana looked wistful. 'Did you like it like that, Nana?' I asked.

She nodded. 'I did. I'm sure my arthritis would be much worse there in the damp and the chill. And my tendency to bronchitis. I'd probably need a walking frame by now, not just a stick, or even…' She paused. 'But most of all, I miss the green.'

Chapter Two

California is called the Golden State. When I was a lot smaller, I once asked my dad if that was because every which way you looked outside of the towns, you saw gold-coloured landscape – gold hills, gold fields dotted with small black cattle grazing gold grass, gold paddocks and meadows and valleys. Dad said no, it was called that because of the Gold Rush, when people discovered there were gold nuggets to be found in the rivers, and many thousands sold up their businesses and left their homes and jobs and families to go west and make their fortunes. Not many did make fortunes, but towns and places were named after the prospectors when they left, which later became famous. And that's why it's the Golden State. He said the gold-coloured landscape is because we don't get enough rain and everything dries up and scorches to a crisp and becomes yellow, especially in summer. That is why we have water rationing, and why there are big fires in the worst droughts, like last year's horrific one, in summer and sometimes all year round. With the bad ones there's a pall of smoke, and ash comes drifting down from the fires many miles away; when we took a trip to Yosemite one time, I saw the burned trees the fires had left behind, mile upon mile of blackened dead stumps, sticking up in ugly jagged spikes against a backdrop of mountains with snow still on them.

Still, I am a California girl born and bred, and I felt I should stick up for my state.

'There's green here too, Nana,' I said, thinking of the smooth green lawns with their sprinklers, the oleanders with pink and white and red flowers lining the freeway for mile after mile, the palm trees, the camellias and bougainvilleas and their glossy green leaves. Even our small town has plenty of green, with shady trees and grassy parks, and in the state capital Sacramento, one hour's drive away, there's even more. My mom and dad take me into Sacramento sometimes, mostly educational visits, to Sutter's Fort or Crocker Art Museum or to Old Sacramento with its boardwalks and saloons and big paddle steamers on the river. There are trees everywhere there. I heard somewhere that Sac has more trees than any other state capital.

'There's plenty of green,' I repeated, as Nana wasn't saying anything. She had a faraway look in her eyes and seemed to give herself a little shake to bring her back into the present. She sighed. 'It's not the same. Back home on the farm, in May and June especially, there's green upon green upon green, piled high and filling every hedgerow, every field, every wood and spinney and verge and meadow with bright fresh green, every twig and branch and stem bursting with new life and seeming to jostle for space. And then there's white as well, cow parsley and stitchwort and creamy may blossom…' She sighed again. 'It was very green that spring,' she said dreamily.

I wanted to know which spring she was talking about, and was opening my mouth to ask when my cell phone buzzed in my backpack, dropped on the patio floor beside my chair. I fumbled for it. Most of my friends keep their cells in their hands all the time, or in a handy pocket, and they're always talking on them, or texting or messaging or playing some game. Me, I think what a waste of time that is, when you could be doing something in the real world, like swimming or horse riding or cycling or reading a book. I wouldn't bother with a cell at all, but Mom makes me promise I'll keep it with me, charged up and switched on at all times, just in case. It was Mom now. 'Juniper? If you've not already left, it's time you were on your way.'

I sighed. It's not like I'm 100 miles away; I only live just round the corner and a few yards down the next street. I can get there in five, or three if I run. But a glance at the clock showed me it was past five already. The afternoon had flown by.

'I have to go,' I said with real regret, and went to give Nana a hug. She hugged me back with arms that were thin but still strong.

'Come again soon. Luciana will be here before long to make sure I'm OK and that I eat dinner.' She pulled a face, as though she wished she wasn't in the position of needing someone to check up on her.

'I will,' I promised, and really meant it, though I didn't know how I was to get time with every waking moment filled – swimming, athletics, horse riding, music, ballet class… although I'm getting too tall for that now, but Mom says it will give me poise. I'd much rather hear about Nana's young days and do without poise. I shouldered my backpack, put on my cap and went out into the baking sun.

On the way home I tried to think what I could give up to be able to see Nana more often. Not swimming, because you just have to swim when it's June and heading for 100 degrees. Mostly I go to one of my friends with a pool, but sometimes to the public pool in town. Not athletics because I'm tall and skinny and good at it. Horse riding, uh-uh. I ride Pimbo, who's a chestnut gelding, and he and I love each other to bits. I could give up cinema visits, maybe, although I do love a good movie, especially an old one with my favourite movie star, Diana (DeeDee) Devine. She has connections with my family in some way I've never been able to figure out. I wouldn't really mind giving up music lessons. I'm tone deaf, and my violin playing sounds like a cat being tortured, my dad says. But Mom makes me stick at it. She wants me to be a well-rounded person, she says. Huh! And I heard her say to one of her friends, 'The way to get them through the adolescent years is to keep them so busy they rush through them without noticing.' Huh again.

Our house is a nice one, single-storey like Nana's but much bigger, set back from our quiet street among shrubs and a live oak, not as jungly as Nana's but nice and shady. It was a relief to get out of the heat into the cool of the air con. Dad was not home yet but Mom was standing by the kitchen island frowning at her phone. She had showered and changed out of her gym kit into shorts and a T-shirt, her week-endy look. Makes her look younger, with her hair pulled out of its chignon and tied back casually. She said, 'Oh, there you are. Just got a text from school.'

I frowned. 'School? On a Saturday?'

She nodded. 'Wouldn't you know it? One week until school's out for summer, and they've gone and got an outbreak of some gastric bug. They're closing early for the summer vacation. Like, now.'

'Oh.' I got a cold cola from the fridge and thought about that. So school was out already. No finishing up of loose ends, no last-minute outings, no goodbyes and plans to meet, no nothing. That was it. School was always mega-careful about *those kinds of bugs and, now I thought about it, three kids had thrown up yesterday. It had been put down to the heat.*

'If anyone needs to bring stuff from school, it can be arranged,' said Mom. 'But that's it.' She paused. 'Makes big problems for us.'

I knew she meant me. Mom and Dad make careful plans around my vacations. But they'd both be working next week. Gran and Gramps were already off on a cruise; my other grandparents live far away in New England.

An idea sprang into my mind. 'I could go to Nana's.'

Mom frowned. 'I don't think Nana is up to child-minding at her age! Short visits yes, but not all day every day for a week.'

'I'm not a child. I'm almost twelve. I can be helpful to her, run errands, fetch things. And Luciana comes in all the time. Please, Mom. I'd like to.'

She looked at me, wavering. 'We-ell – I could ask her. But won't it be dull for you, cooped up with an old lady…'

'No,' I said. 'I like to be with Nana. Really. She's been telling me about when she was young. And I really, really, want to know more about her life.'

Chapter Three

There was some kind of argument going on when Dad came home from work. He had done some accounts at the office, and I was in bed by then. I'd been reading a book on careers, and when I put it down and switched off the light I lay there thinking for a while. I just could not make up my mind what I wanted to do with my life. Mom and Dad always tell me I should fly high and go for anything I want, that I could aim to be president of the United States if I want to. Uh-uh! Who would want all that responsibility and constantly having to shake people's hands and pretend to be nice? I like people but I like my own space as well. The trouble was, I couldn't decide what I did want to do, or even what college courses to aim for. Professional sport? I like sport but only as relaxation. Something with animals? Maybe. Teaching? Another maybe, especially if it was teaching English. I love books. But I wasn't sure about that either.

Mom and Dad don't usually argue; they make the most of the time they have together. Their voices were not raised, but there was definitely a tone of disagreement to their conversation now. When I heard my name mentioned I got out of bed, creeping down the passage to the corner of the wing leading to the living space, where I could listen.

'It doesn't seem right for a child of her age to be in that situation,' said Mom. I could imagine how her mouth would be set in a stubborn line. 'What if something happened? It's not fair on Juniper.'

Dad laughed and I knew his eyes would be crinkling up at the corners. 'Juni's a sensible girl. Nothing will happen. Luciana is in and out. And it's in the very early stages yet.'

'But it will get worse. We don't know how soon. Anything could happen.'

'Unlikely in just a week. Let her go. She's fond of Nana.'

My heart had begun to thump hard. Nana was ill, that's what they meant. It must be something very serious – she must be dying...

I sprang round the corner and confronted them. They were standing by the kitchen island and both jumped. Mom said, 'Juni! I thought you were asleep!'

'Well, I wasn't. What's wrong with Nana? Is she going to die?'

I realised as I spoke what a silly question that was. Nana was almost ninety, after all. But I couldn't bear the thought of losing her, and felt tears spring to my eyes. Dad reached out a long arm and drew me in. He had showered at the office and smelled of soap and aftershave. 'Calm down, Juni. No, she isn't – well, hopefully not for a while.'

I pulled away. 'Then what? There's something. I heard you. Tell me!'

They looked at each other. Mom sighed, and said, 'I guess we'd better come clean, Pete. Sit down, Juniper.'

I perched on the arm of the big chair. Mom and Dad sat down too.

'Look, Juni, it's like this. Nana isn't physically ill exactly, but she has something called dementia.'

'What's that?'

'It's – well, it's a kind of degeneration of the brain. Mostly it's elderly people that get it, but sometimes younger ones too. People start to lose their memory and get muddled with faces and names and places, then they start to forget things like how to use appliances, which can be very dangerous. They get confused if they're in different places, and forget how to get home, and even in time forget their own family members.'

I started to protest. It couldn't be true. Nana had a wonderful memory; why, only this afternoon she'd been remembering things from way back in her childhood, the farm she'd lived on and even the weather there – but then I remembered a couple of weeks ago she'd woken from one of her little naps and called me Margaret. Margaret is her daughter, my gran. Gran is nothing like me either; her hair is dyed blonde at present but it had been light brown once, whereas mine is dark like Mom's. I'm tall and skinny, while I'd seen pictures of Gran as a plump, stocky little girl. Nana had called me Margaret for a while before she seemed to remember.

It must be true. I burst into tears.

I don't cry often and they were concerned. 'You don't have to go there next week, honey,' said Mom. 'We can make other arrangements.'

I pulled myself together. 'I want to go! Don't try and stop me! I'm going!'

I felt a lump of sadness in my chest when I got to Nana's on Monday morning. Luciana was there, putting the vacuum away. The house was neat, Nana sitting out on the back porch with Megan on her lap. She looked the same as usual, long cotton skirt, shady pink hat, all serene. Surely there had been a mistake. I had a quick word with Luciana before going out to her. 'Luciana, is it true? About the – the dementia?'

Luciana's kind, plump face got serious. 'It's true, honey. I'm glad they told you. She's much as usual, your nana, just a little lapse now and then. Just love on her the same as usual. Lunch is all ready in the ice box. And don't forget to call if you need me. I can be here in a blink.'

I felt comforted, and gave Luciana a hug. Nana was pleased to see me. I hugged her too, and felt how frail her shoulder blades seemed under her cotton shirt. Megan jumped down and gave me a look. I think she liked having Nana all to herself. She went off huffily to the shade of the oleander.

I sat down in the opposite chair. Nana pushed up her shades and looked at me with her blue-grey eyes. She said quietly, 'You don't have to whisper in corners with Luciana. I know.'

My heart gave a painful jolt. I knew immediately what she meant. She knew about the cruel thing that was happening to her mind, and what would happen later. And she knew I knew. I felt tears spring to my eyes and blinked them away. 'I'm sorry, Nana.'

She smiled, her eyes disappearing in wrinkles as they always did. 'Don't be sorry. I've had a long life, a good life, oh, I've been so blessed! And I may beat this thing yet. I may just pop off before it gets a real grip. Now wouldn't that be a laugh?'

She actually did laugh. Then she said, 'But even if that doesn't happen, even if I get confused and forget you all and my *mind goes, remember one thing, Juni. I'm not just body and mind, none of us is. We have a spirit too, and our spirit is the real person, the real us, the part that makes us who we are, the part that goes back to God when this life ends. And remember this too, even if my mind has gone, and this old body wears out and lets me down, my spirit goes on straight and will go on forever.'*

I felt tingles go up and down my spine. I knew Nana believed in God and that she read her battered old Bible with big print, but hearing her say those things brought a real sense of comfort. And a kind of awe. My friends and me say 'awesome' all the time, but this was the real deal. I felt myself relax and a burden lift.

'Now then,' said Nana, leaning forward and putting her shades back on. 'We have a whole week! What shall we do?'

I knew what I wanted. 'Nana, you started telling me about when you were my age the other day. Could you tell me some more?'

Then I could have bitten my tongue, and I thought, how awful if she can't remember and gets confused and upset. But then I saw she had a big smile on her face. 'I was hoping you'd say that! You know, Juni, if I tell you about those times, maybe some day you could write it all down so it won't be forgotten.'

And then I knew, all in the blink of an eye, that I would. And more than that, that I needn't puzzle any more about what I wanted to do with my life, and that what I wanted most in the whole world was to be a writer. And I would start with Nana's memories. 'Yes!' I said.

'Right then, let's go. We have drinks there on the table. It's not too hot yet. Where shall we start?'

'You said, last time, about one spring when it was very green. You said about how green it always was, every spring, on the farm where you were born, but there was one time especially…'

'Oh yes. But that's not quite how it was. I wasn't born on the farm at all, or even in the country. I was born in London.'

Chapter Four

June

The house we lived in was a two-up, two-down mid-terrace in Greenwich, south-east London. We had a little backyard, where Mum tried to grow marigolds and petunias, until the war came and we dug it all up to plant potatoes. 'Dig for Victory' was one of the slogans we saw everywhere, along with 'Be like Dad, keep Mum' and 'Careless Talk Costs Lives' which were meant to be warnings to watch what we said in case an enemy spy might be listening. 'Walls Have Ears' was another one. I didn't understand what any of them meant; I was nine when the war started and a lot of the talk went over my head… the Second World War, you know, against Hitler and the Nazis. Dad worked at the docks before the war, and Mum worked in a bakery, which was good, because she was allowed to bring home some of the unsold bread and buns and cakes at the end of the day. It was always a nice surprise to see what she brought, and a disappointment if they'd sold out. My favourites were cream buns.

We had a WC that we had to share with several other families, and a wash house at the back which housed the washtubs and mangle, and the tin bath hanging on a nail which Mum took down on Saturday nights for my weekly bath by the kitchen fire. After school, I went to Mrs Wilkins' next door for an hour until Mum came home, or played in the street with the other kids.

I was an only child. Most families in the street had a lot of kids, and I longed for brothers and sisters, or even just one sibling, but when I was old enough to understand, Mum told me that something had gone wrong at my birth and she could not have more children. Some of the other kids at school envied me, especially girls my age who often had to look after smaller brothers and sisters. I envied them; I'd have loved a little one to take care of, and I sometimes 'borrowed' a toddler to carry about or push around in a little cart. We couldn't have a dog either, because both my parents were at work all day and it wouldn't have been fair on it. We did have a cat, because cats are independent creatures and come and go as they please. He was black with a white tip to his tail and four white feet that looked like little boots, so 'Boots' he became.

Things changed when the war came. Dad and Mum and everyone else looked serious all the time, and one day Dad came home looking like a stranger in a khaki uniform. Mum tried to be brave when he went off to the army but I knew she cried every night. Sometimes I crept into her room and got into bed with her, and then we ended up sleeping together in the big bed all the time, except when Dad came home on leave.

He came a few times, and what excitement there was when we knew he was coming. Mum would save our rations of sugar and butter and dried fruit and would make a yummy fruit cake, and she'd do her best to find a nice piece of beef or a chicken for roasting. She'd dig out one of her pretty dresses from before the war, and get our neighbour to set her hair for her, and she'd put on lipstick and perfume. I think she'd have liked to go to the pictures or dancing, war or no war, but Dad seemed tired, and just wanted to sit listening to the wireless or pottering in the garden or doing ordinary things. But it was lovely to have him home, just to have him reading a bedtime story to me and tucking me in as he always had, and the time always flew by too quickly. Mum would be sad and quiet for a few days after he'd gone.

When the bombing started it was a shock to everyone. We heard the crump of bombs down at the docks and saw the orange flare of fires. The docks were not all that far away, and the next bombs might be even closer. Some people had bomb shelters, ugly concrete boxes roofed with thick concrete slabs, or steel Anderson shelters, but we did not, so every time the sirens wailed Mum and I joined the rest of the population of the nearby streets hurrying to the railway arch at the end of our road, clutching what pillows, blankets and other goods we'd had time to grab. There we made ourselves as comfortable as we could until the all-clear sounded. We didn't sleep much, most nights. People swapped stories with one another, strangers quickly became friends. Sometimes there was an enterprising person who would organise a sing-song, belting out the old favourites like 'Knees Up Mother Brown' and 'Roll Out the Barrel'. Not that there was any room for a knees-up and dancing, but the cheery tunes kept up our spirits as we huddled in our eiderdowns.

There had already been a first wave of children being sent away from London to the safety of the countryside, even before the bombing started in earnest. Mum had tentatively considered putting my name down to go with my school, but the thought terrified me. Whatever happened, I wanted to stay with Mum. I begged and pleaded, and she relented. Some of the children had even returned when nothing much seemed to be happening. But now there was bombing almost every night, with the crump and boom and flash of the bombs sometimes at a distance, sometimes much nearer, and the fires turning the night sky pink and orange. I could see she was more and more anxious. Then the terrible morning came when, blinking eyes that smarted with tiredness, we emerged from the shelter to find that our street had taken a direct hit and the houses at the other end had been reduced to rubble. We did not know what had happened to the people inside, whether they'd got to the shelter or not. We knew that a middle-aged couple lived in one, and an elderly man with his sister in another. But, clinging together and picking our way through scattered rubble towards home, I saw something that made me turn cold with horror. I screamed. The body of a black cat lay half-buried under a pile of stone and cement and plaster. Its front half could not be seen, but I recognised the white hind feet and the white tip to the tail. I clutched Mum. 'It's Boots!'

I darted forward to try to pull him out, but Mum held me back. 'He's dead, sweetie. We can't do anything. Let's get home and see if there's gas for a cup of tea.'

An air raid warden in uniform and tin hat was coming towards us. 'Sorry, missus, houses in this street may not be safe. You'll have to go along to the church hall and wait while they're checked.'

It was soon afterwards that Mum told me I would be leaving with the next wave of evacuees.

Chapter Five

There was a crowd of kids that day, milling about on the station platform, all ages, from teens down to tiny tots. These little ones mostly had their mums with them and were probably the most secure of us all, bewildered by all that was going on, but safe in the knowledge of Mum close by. Most of the others were apprehensive, unsure, some tearful, some (mostly boys) excited at the idea of a new adventure and the novelty of a long train journey. A few harassed teachers and helpers worked hard trying to keep everyone together, and safe.

It was a chilly autumn day, grey and foggy, and all of us were wearing our winter coats and a hat of some kind. All of us also had our gas masks in their cardboard cases round our necks, our names on labels pinned to our coats, and were clutching suitcases. I had my own small suitcase, packed lovingly by Mum, with a few tears when she thought I wasn't noticing. She had put in my woollen jerseys, warm underclothing, knitted socks, washing things and a hot-water bottle. 'It's sure to be a bit chilly out there in the country,' she said briskly. 'But think what fun it will be if it snows. Snowmen and sledging, all kinds of fun…'

I wasn't convinced. 'I don't want to go,' I said stubbornly. 'I want to stay with you. I don't mind the bombs, honest. It's fun down in the shelter…'

My voice tailed off. It wasn't fun. I was scared nearly all the time of that wailing siren and the rush down the street in the darkness. I was terrified of the crump of bombs, the fires that turned the sky pink and showed up as far away as Dover, I'd been told. There hadn't been another hit in our area. That one had been a stray event, everyone said so, they were targeting the munitions factories, the government places where important things were decided, the docks. I didn't believe that it wouldn't happen again. I hardly knew what to believe. Everything was topsy-turvy and I lived in fear every day.

But the greatest fear of all was the fear of being separated from my mum. 'Can't you come too?' I pleaded, but she shook her head. 'Only the under-fives go with their mothers. I'll stay here as long as the bakery stays open. And I want to be here when your dad comes home again. He'll be so happy to know you're in a safe place. I'll write and I'll come and visit, promise.'

The station name was painted over, but there were posters up on the walls. 'Is Your Journey Really Necessary?' and 'Leave Hitler to me sonny, YOU ought to be out of London'. I saw two of our teachers from school, Miss Grey and Miss Adams, going around trying to keep the children together, take them to the toilet along the platform, comfort the weeping ones and generally maintain some kind of order. There was a stirring of excitement when the train came hissing and steaming down the track and drew to a halt at the platform. The doors opened and children were beginning to be ushered inside, one of the ladies with an armband ticking off names on a list.

It was then that I lost control. I looked at my mum's white face, lips set in a line as she tried bravely to smile, and burst into tears, flinging myself at her and clutching at her coat. 'I won't go, I won't!'

Poor Mum, she must have been at her wits' end as she tried desperately to dislodge my clinging fingers. 'Sweetie, you have to. Look there's Miss Grey – and Marjorie from your class – come on, you're a big girl now…'

I didn't care. I wasn't going. It was Miss Adams who saved the day. She came pushing through the crowd towards us, holding a small child by the hand. 'Now, June, what's all this? Come along now, I have a special job for you. This is Freddie from the infants' class, and he's on his own. His mum…' she gave Mum a look and murmured something I couldn't hear, which told me something very bad must have happened to his mum. 'Anyway, he's not quite five and needs someone to take care of him. I think you're just what he needs.'

Miss Adams knew me well. Her request was the one thing that would calm my hysterics and give me purpose. I looked at Freddie, a sad waif who obviously came from one of the poorer neighbourhoods. His clothes looked too big for him, he had on boots but no socks and he was skinny; his thin little legs had a look of rickets. He held a small battered suitcase. Sad blue eyes looked up at me from a grimy face under a thatch of blond hair. His lower lip wobbled. Miss Adams took my hand and wrapped it around Freddie's. 'There. June will take good care of you, Freddie.'

That grubby little hand clung to mine as though his life depended on it. Miss Adams gave a sigh of relief and patted my shoulder. She patted Mum's too, and went off to see to someone else. Children were still clambering onto the train. I was suddenly calm, the tears drying on my cheeks, although I saw fresh ones in Mum's eyes. She gave me a last hug, said she would write as soon as she had an address, and reminded me there was paper and pencil in my case to write to her. Then Freddie and I were climbing on the train, almost the last to board. A marshal hurried us along as the doors began to close. I had one last look at Mum, a lone figure waving a handkerchief among a sea of fluttering white hankies, as there came a hissing of steam and we were off.

The journey seemed long, endless. Buildings flashed by the windows for mile after mile, stations with names painted over and then, even more endless, we travelled through countryside, green and brown fields, trees in autumn colours, villages, more fields. The train seemed full of restless children, fidgeting, sniffing, poking each other, getting up and sitting down again, endlessly asking the weary helpers, 'Miss, are we nearly there yet?'

The compartments were packed, some faces blackened with smuts from leaning out of the windows, although they were strictly warned not to do so. Some were tearful, some nervous and quiet, others inclined to quarrel. Some sobbed quietly, some wet themselves, at least half a dozen were sick. There was a smell of sweaty feet and unwashed bodies and damp clothing. The one toilet down the corridor was smelly too, but I heard Miss Grey remark to Miss Adams that thank heaven there was a toilet; not all trains had them. We were given corned beef sandwiches and lemonade to drink until it ran out, and then we had water. The helpers escorted endless infants to the toilet, comforted the sad ones, tried to calm the overexuberant, reprimanded the naughty ones. All the time, Freddie sat close beside me, his sticky hand clutching mine until I needed it to eat my sandwiches, and then he held onto my coat pocket. From time to time his big blue eyes looked up at me, and I managed to smile at him. He didn't smile back, but I could tell I was now his refuge, his safe place. I wiped his nose, held his drink for him, took him to the toilet. A helper that I didn't know looked in on our compartment and said, 'He's a good little chap, isn't he, your brother? Not like some, I'm afraid.'

I didn't enlighten her. I'd always wanted a little brother. Freddie didn't seem to have family, so I would be his family, his big sister. We could be billeted together; they did try to keep families together, I'd heard. I'd take care of him. My spirits rose.

The train travelled on, rattling over the rails, tickety-tack, tickety-tack. Most of us dozed. Freddie slept, lying across my lap, his little body hot and sticky. Some whimpered in their sleep; now and then there'd be a confused voice calling for Mum.

Then I awoke from a doze with the sudden realisation that something had changed. The rhythm had slowed, the whistle blew, steam hissed as brakes were applied; we were pulling into a station. I looked out to see people there waiting. Waiting for us, for we children were the only people on the train. We had arrived.

Chapter Six

There were women in the dark green uniforms of the Women's Voluntary Service waiting to meet us on the small country platform, its name covered like all the others with white paint. Dazed, crumpled and travel stained, we were ushered off the train, blinking around us in bewilderment. Freddie's fingers clutched tight to mine, our gas masks in their carriers hung from our necks, and we clung onto our small possessions. All this time, Freddie had hardly spoken a word, except for a whispered yes or no when asked if he was hungry or thirsty or needed the WC. We trooped out of the station, following our teachers and the other ladies into a quiet village street and then crossing the road to a large building by itself. Inside, long tables were set out with plates of sandwiches and buns and cakes and jugs of lemonade. More ladies fussed with tea urns at one end.

Miss Adams and Miss Grey marshalled their flock once again, counted us, ticked off our names on another list and told us in determinedly cheerful voices that we would be having tea here before being collected to go to our new homes. A stout lady clapped her hands to silence any chatter, and then said grace.

'Dear Lord, thank you for the safe arrival among us of these poor dear children. We pray your blessing upon them and upon your bountiful provision for us.'

Our weariness dropped away as we fell on the food with a vengeance. I got a plate of sandwiches and buns for Freddie and poured him lemonade.

He looked bewildered, but when I began to eat, he ate too, as though he hadn't seen food for a long time. In fact, we all stuffed ourselves full as though none of us had eaten for days. I heard one helper murmur, 'Poor little mites, they seem to be half-starved.' And another reply, 'It's what they might have brought with them that worries me! Riddled with head lice, I shouldn't wonder.'

They spoke in accents very different to our own, but I had no difficulty understanding them. I almost choked with indignation. Half-starved? Head lice? I turned and glared at her round red face and she realised I'd heard and turned away, her face a few shades redder. I wanted to shout, 'I've always had lots to eat! Roast beef, and bubble-and-squeak, and fish and chips on Saturday nights! And I haven't got head lice; dirty people get them!' My mother was very fussy about that, unplaiting my long hair and going through it with a nit-comb every bath night. She'd be mortified. But then, I'd seen some of the others scratch their heads now and then. And some, like poor little Freddie with his rickety legs, did look half-starved. And he was stuffing his food in with both hands, as though he didn't know when he'd get any more.

When we'd eaten everything, the trestle tables were quickly cleared and taken down, and chairs arranged along one side of the hall. We wondered what was coming next. We soon found out, as people began to arrive, women and one or two men, a few children with some of them. These were the families that we'd be billeted with. We huddled together and looked apprehensively at them, trying to work out which ones looked kind, and hoping we'd be with the nice ones.

It seemed very strange when some of the people began to point and speak to those in charge. 'I can take three girls, if they don't mind sharing, those three maybe,' said a woman. Others began to point out children and say what they wanted. A man in gaiters said, 'I could do with a good strong lad to help out on the farm,' and an elderly lady said she'd take one little girl, if she seemed well behaved. The people in charge were trying hard to keep family groups together, not always an easy task, but slowly the waiting crowd of children grew less and so did the prospective host families, as evacuees and their hosts left together, hopefully well matched.

A youngish couple approached us; they were well dressed and smiling. The woman looked at Freddie and her eyes sparkled. 'Oh, what a little sweetheart! Such beautiful eyes! Poor little soul! We'll take him, won't we, darling?' She clasped her hands and looked appealingly at her husband. I wondered why he was not in uniform. Both of them seemed to have rather posh accents. Her offer clearly did not include me. I stepped forward quickly, holding tight to Freddie's clutching hand. 'He's my brother. We have to stay together.'

The woman looked at my belligerent expression and her face clouded. Freddie clutched me tightly. 'Oh,' she said. 'I'm afraid we can only manage one.'

Miss Grey was coming across, tut-tutting. 'June, what is this nonsense? You and Freddie are not brother and sister! You've just been taking care of him for the journey!' She turned to the couple. 'I'm sure he'd love to go with you, wouldn't you, Freddie?'

Freddie began to cry, large tears rolling down his grubby cheeks. He clung on to me with both hands. I glared at Miss Grey and the couple. Miss Grey was trying to dislodge Freddie's sticky fingers, and finally succeeded. The woman took him by the hand and began to lead him away. He burst into loud wailing and found his voice at last. 'June! June! I want to stay with June! June! Joo-oon!' He was led firmly away, his wails getting fainter in the distance. I had tears in my own eyes. I'd depended on Freddie too; in a way he really had become my little brother, my family on this long, strange, unfamiliar day of travelling. I realised I needed him.

Miss Grey was losing patience. 'I really don't know what's got into you, June. You're usually a sensible girl!' Poor woman, she must have been every bit as tired and frazzled as we were. She sighed with relief when an untidy, harassed-looking woman headed our way and looked me over. 'I'll take this girl. Would you like to come with me, dear? We live on a farm. My name's Mrs Powell.'

I didn't want to go with anyone. I wanted my own mum, and home, and everything I knew. I wanted to curl up in a ball and cry. But I was introduced and before I knew it, urged on by Miss Grey, I was picking up my case and following Mrs Powell out of the hall, with Freddie's wails still ringing in my ears.

Interlude

Juniper

So engrossed was I in the world of Nana's childhood, when bombs fell on city streets and children were sent away from their homes, that I jumped when Luciana slid back the patio door and came out on the back porch.

'It's past lunchtime. It's already set out for you both. You must be ready for it.'

I blinked, leaving the world of the bleak British countryside and returning to one where the sun blazed from a cloudless sky and green fruit was ripening on the orange and lemon trees. Nana took a long drink from the glass beside her. 'Do you know, I hardly noticed the time passing. I was right back there. Thank you, Luciana.'

Luciana smiled and said, 'I'll leave you to eat. Back later.'

I said, 'Me too, Nana. How dreadful to be parted from your family and sent off to live with strangers. Thank goodness things like that don't happen here and now.'

Nana was thoughtful. 'Oh, but they do, Juni. Think of the immigrants, legal and illegal. People like Luis and Luciana and Mateo, people who are desperate for a better life. And then those in other countries fearful of war and persecution and torture and famine, fearful for their very lives. The cruel disappointment when other countries won't take them in. We are the fortunate ones, Juni, but we have a duty to those less fortunate. Never forget that.'

I took a drink too and thought about it. I remembered the homeless people we saw everywhere, especially in big cities like San Francisco and Sacramento. I'd seen them begging in the streets, rifling through Goodwill bins, whole families with kids living in cardboard shacks by the roadside. Some lived in the bushes along the riverbank, concealed from the police, along with the rattlesnakes and the mosquitoes. California is the perfect place to be homeless, my dad says, mild all year round. He sometimes gives change to youngsters begging from vehicles that have to stop at intersections, but sometimes he's sceptical. 'Notice many of those panhandlers, their good cell phones and expensive backpacks and sneakers?' And Mom says, 'Yes, but how awful to have to beg, and to have no home.'

I thought of our home, with shining wood floors, sparkling white kitchen, comfortable beds, cool air conditioning. So different from the lives of the homeless and the refugees. Different too from Nana's childhood in a tiny house with the bathroom in the backyard. Nana's house here is smaller than ours, but it has everything that ours has. I wondered for the first time how Nana had come to America in the first place. Maybe she would tell me as her story went on. I was curious first of all to find how she had liked the home and family at the farm she had gone to.

She must have read my thoughts, because she said, reaching for her stick, 'Let's go in and have some lunch. I'm quite hungry after all that talking. Then I think I'll take a little nap. Maybe you'd like one too. But then, if you like, we can go on with the story.'

Chapter Seven

June

We got into a battered-looking farm truck, Mrs Powell stowing my case in the back along with various sacks, boxes, odd machinery parts and muddy boots. She climbed into the driving seat. Her face looked tanned and weather-beaten, she wore trousers, an old waterproof coat and shapeless woolly hat, her feet in Wellington boots. She must have seen me looking, because she said, 'I had to come just as I was, no time to change. Had to pick up basic slag from the farmers' co-op. Did I tell you we live on a farm? My husband wasn't in from work; it's potato picking time. We grow a lot of potatoes these days, doesn't go down well with him at all. War Ag, you know.'

I was silent, trying to digest all this. I had no idea what the War Ag might be. I'd never heard of basic slag. I was going to a farm. I'd never been to one before, didn't have a clue what it might be like. Silly verses from the 'Old MacDonald' song went through my head.

'Did you have a good journey?' enquired Mrs Powell, putting the truck into gear with a rasping sound and heading out into the village street.

I nodded and said, 'Yes, thanks,' although I was still smarting from the scene with Freddie, and I thought the whole journey had been pretty horrible. I was tired out and I wanted to cry, so I pressed my lips tightly together and blinked hard, determined I wouldn't. Mrs Powell drove out of the village and into the open countryside between empty fields and trees still with leaves clinging to them. Drifts of coloured leaves lay piled at either side of the road. Mrs Powell drove at what seemed like breakneck speed, and I found myself clutching the sides of the seat. Dusk was falling, it would be quite dark in a short while.

'Back before dark if we look sharp,' said Mrs Powell. 'Can't stand driving if we have to use those brownouts to dim the headlights.' She must have noticed my mystified look, because she went on: 'Like blackout, but only partly so as to leave some light.' Another pause. 'You'll meet the rest of the family.' She glanced at me again. 'You're a quiet one, aren't you? You needn't be shy with us, we're very easy-going.'

I couldn't tell her that I was not shy, just lonely, and bewildered, and sad, and heartbroken, that I wanted my mum and dad, and for everything to be the same as it was before this horrible war.

We drove for a while along quiet, empty roads before climbing a hill and then turning into a narrow, rutted, bumpy lane, with big potholes that Mrs Powell swerved around in a scary way. I was beginning to feel sick and wished I hadn't eaten quite so many egg sandwiches and buns at the village hall. Mrs Powell did not slacken her speed, so it was a relief when we bounced and swerved our way around a corner and drew to a halt in a darkening farmyard where a house and outbuildings loomed suddenly before us. A slit of light immediately showed from a darkened window and several faces peered out.

Mrs Powell grabbed my case from the back seat and opened the door.

'Here we are! Come along, mind the mud, let's get inside.'

The air felt cold and raw and it was indeed muddy. I felt my best shoes squish into it as I followed Mrs Powell. She ushered me into a large, warm, lamplit room that seemed full of people. A couple of cats, a ginger and a tabby, slept curled up together on one of the chairs by the fire.

Mrs Powell had pulled off her boots and shed her coat and hat as we went in, revealing a head of untidy greying hair. 'Here we are! This is June, she's from London, so let's make her welcome! Come to the fire, love.'

She ushered me to the chair where the cats were and shooed them off onto the floor, where they glared resentfully at us both. The fire was burning in a black range, with what appeared to be an oven at one side and a boiler at the other. Several pairs of eyes regarded me curiously. Mrs Powell was tying on a flowered pinafore over her jumper and trousers. 'Now then, dear, this is my husband, Mr Powell, and these are our youngsters, Sylvia, Tom and Annie.' She began to bustle about, suspending a big black kettle from a hook over the fire, bringing a large loaf from a cupboard and beginning to slice it. 'Sylvia, go and fetch the milk and butter from the dairy. And a piece of cheese. Oh, and that dish of beetroot and onions we did yesterday. And the ham. Annie, clear the table and set it for supper – don't forget the extra place. Tom, stop gawping and fetch a couple more logs.'

I watched the family as they set about their tasks, feeling awkward, as though I should be doing something myself. They had all said 'Hello' politely enough, and Mr Powell had shaken hands. The oldest girl, Sylvia, I guessed would be fifteen or sixteen, blonde and very pretty, wearing dungarees and a jersey, her hair tied back with a red scarf. The boy and the other girl looked about the same size, and I wondered if they might be twins, although they did not look at all alike. The boy was thin and dark, with a narrow face, the girl fair-haired, though not as blonde as her sister. She had an inquisitive, eager expression and a sprinkling of freckles across her nose. I noticed that she and her brother both had the same colour eyes, green with flecks of hazel, and long lashes. The father was dark and wiry like his son; after the initial greetings he did not say much, but buried his head in the pages of a paper called the *Farmer and Stockbreeder*.

As soon as they'd got over the first awkwardness, the three children clustered around me, plying me with questions. Sylvia sounded almost envious. 'It must be fun, living in London with all the shops and the cinema and the West End and everything. I love the cinema, don't you? Gary Cooper and Greer Garson are my favourite film stars, which ones do you like? And Clark Gable, he's dreamy! Have you seen *It Happened One Night*?'

I shook my head. I'd only been to the pictures once or twice, and not at all since the war started.

'Did you get bombed?' asked Tom, his eyes gleaming with excitement. 'What's it like? Can you see the planes? Can you see the swastikas on them?'

I couldn't help a shudder. Bombs and planes were the last thing I wanted to talk about. In fact, I didn't want to talk at all. Mrs Powell came to my rescue. 'Let the poor girl be, she must be worn out! Supper's ready, come and have it.'

We sat around the big table in the middle of the kitchen, eating juicy pink ham, beetroot and onions in vinegar, crusty bread with real farmhouse butter, a big wedge of cheese, and apple tart. My eyes grew round at the amount of food on the table, and nobody portioning out our rations. I guiltily remembered that I hadn't yet handed over my blue ration book to Mrs Powell. She must have guessed my thoughts, because she said, 'We are very fortunate with food here on the farm. We grow our own fruit and veg, we keep a pig, we have hens for eggs, a couple of cows for milk and butter and cheese. Of course, we have to hand over a lot to the government, but I make sure we all have enough. I bake my own bread. It must be so hard on people in towns, with rationing and all.'

I said, 'I'm sorry, I forgot to give you my ration book.'

She smiled and said, 'That's all right, my love, don't you fret. Have a bit more tart. Have as much as you want.'

I already felt stuffed so full I was beginning to feel sick again, what with the tea at the village hall and now another big meal. I said, 'No, thank you,' and added quickly, 'It was lovely.'

She nodded approvingly, seeming rather surprised by my politeness. I wondered if they'd expected all of us evacuees to be rude and unmannerly. I remembered what I'd overheard about head lice, and suddenly felt overwhelmed with homesickness. Despite Mrs Powell's kindness, I was a stranger who'd just been dumped on them, like all the others. I wondered how poor little Freddie was getting on, and felt the tears spring to my eyes again.

I learned that there was no WC here, just an outhouse across the garden, shaded by a lilac tree. Annie accompanied me with a torch and waited outside to escort me back. There were mysterious shrubs and bushes that brushed against us along the garden path and I shivered, imagining clutching fingers. An owl hooted somewhere close by, making me jump. It was eerily quiet, no hum of traffic, no sounds from other houses because there were no other houses, not even the occasional dog yapping, although that was a rare sound nowadays. No planes and sirens. I should have been glad of that, but all I felt was a cold loneliness.

I was shown to the room I was to share with Annie, containing two beds with patchwork quilts, lit by a candle in a tin holder. They left me to undress and I did so quickly, getting into bed and blowing out the candle. When Annie came to bed, with her mother looking in to check on me, I pretended to be asleep. 'Poor lamb, she's worn out,' said Mrs Powell in a whisper. 'Let her sleep, Annie, don't start your chattering. Plenty of time for that.'

But I was still awake long after Annie had got into bed and was gently snoring, my eyes stinging with unshed tears. When I was sure she was sound asleep, I pulled the covers over my head and sobbed into my pillow.

Chapter Eight

I woke next morning to a sense of bewilderment, not knowing for a moment where I was, with no morning sounds of the clatter of people in the street and the hum of the big city. No traffic sounds, no sirens, no bombs. It was late, Annie's bed empty, the patchwork quilt thrown back. I felt rested, and thought maybe it would be all right here, if it wasn't for the ache of not having Mum.

I got out of bed and went to the window, drawing back the thick curtains. Even in the country they had blackout, it seemed. The light inside the room was grey and dim, and just as grey outside, a gloomy, overcast, raw-looking autumn day. Leafless trees clustered round the stark grey stone farm buildings, stretching their bare branches towards a gunmetal-grey sky. Beyond were fields of a sludgy greenish brown. The farmyard itself was a sea of mud, the same brownish clay-like mud that had dried on my shoes overnight. A couple of cows stood dejectedly inside the gate of the nearest field, their feet in churned-up mud that sucked at their hooves as they turned away and began to graze on what grass they could find. A big black crow cawed and flapped in one of the trees. I felt my heart sink like a stone.

Annie came bursting into the room as I was getting dressed. She surveyed my jumper and skirt critically, and tossed a pair of dungarees onto my bed. 'Here. Better put these on. Don't want to mess up your good clothes.' She was in identical dungarees, and a jersey with darns on the elbows. In the daylight her hair had a gingerish tinge, and her freckles stood out. She said, 'You can help me with my Saturday jobs, after breakfast.'

I had Saturday jobs back home, tidying my bedroom and hanging up clothes. At least it would be something to do. We got our own breakfast, helping ourselves to porridge that stood in a saucepan on the hob with, to my amazement, thick cream and brown sugar. I had not tasted anything so delicious for a long time. Nobody else seemed to be about.

'Mum's doing the milking,' said Annie, with her mouth full. 'Dad's out in the potato field and Tom's helping. Sylvia's gone to the village.'

I was mystified. I knew milk came from cows, unlike some in my school who thought it was made in factories. But it had never occurred to me that the milk had to be extracted from the cows by someone, and particularly not by a woman. But before we had finished eating, the door in the adjoining scullery opened, and Annie's mother came in on a breath of cold air, dressed in a raggedy old coat and Wellington boots, carrying a bucket in each hand. She peered in at us, her cheeks red under a woolly hat that looked like a tea cosy. 'Ah, you're up, dear. I hope Annie's taking good care of you. Busy day ahead.'

She disappeared into a room beyond the scullery with the buckets. I heard metallic clanking sounds.

'That's the dairy,' explained Annie. 'Let's get out of here quick, or she'll get us to work the separator, and I hate that. Makes your arm ache and takes ages.'

I had no idea what a separator might be. We piled our dishes into the stone sink and Annie found me a pair of boots and an old jacket. We went out into the chilly grey day, a damp kind of cold that made me shiver.

In a field beyond the farm yard I could see Mr Powell and his son, bending over rows of turned earth, picking up something and putting it into sacks. A cart stood near the gate.

'Potato picking, ugh!' said Annie. She collected two pitchforks and a wheelbarrow from an outhouse and gave me one of the forks. I wondered what the Saturday job could be. I soon found out. She led the way to the edge of the yard where a wooden hut stood, and flung open the door.

'Fowl house to clean out!' she announced, and grinned at my surprised face. 'Don't look so scared. It's better than cleaning the goose shed. Or the pigsty.' She held her nose to show how smelly those would be. 'Come on, the two of us will soon get it done.'

It was bad enough, I thought. The chickens were out, pecking around in the mud outside in a half-hearted kind of way, but they had left behind a thick layer of droppings and dirty straw, which when disturbed by our forks gave off a sharp, unpleasant acrid smell that stung my nose and made my eyes water. It wasn't the Saturday job I'd expected. Reluctantly I did as Annie did, forking the stuff off the floor and dumping it in the wheelbarrow. The stench grew worse and worse. It must have been ages since it was last cleaned. I hadn't expected to be doing farm work. By the time we'd finished and put down a layer of fresh straw, I was aching and feeling a stirring of resentment.

Tom's face appeared round the corner of the shed as we finished tipping the last contents of the wheelbarrow onto the manure heap in the yard. He gave a sniggering kind of laugh. 'Having fun, girls?'

'More fun than you, Shorty,' retorted Annie, and flicked a blob of chicken muck from the end of her fork in his direction. It missed, but he picked up my discarded fork and flicked a blob back. That missed her too, but I wasn't quite quick enough, and caught the blob on my cheek. I gave a snort of disgust, wiped off the mess on my jacket sleeve and glared at him. What a horrible boy! The whole place was horrible, the mud, the stinky chicken poo, and I hated it all. He was grinning at me in an infuriating way. 'Ooops, sorry, Miss Fancy Townie. But that's what you get round here – mud, and muck.'

I was tempted to throw something back at him. But he was gone, round the corner with another laugh. Annie had a smile on her face too, but she said quickly, 'Don't take any notice of him. He's a dope. Just because he's two years older than me and we're the same size, he takes it out on me. I can't help it if he's got little short legs. Mum says he'll suddenly shoot up, that's what boys do, but I reckon he'll always be a titch. Have you got brothers and sisters?'

I shook my head bleakly. 'No. Just me.'

'You're lucky, then. I wish I hadn't. Sylvia's always bossing me about and all she thinks about is clothes and hairstyles and how she wishes she could be a film star. And Tom – well…' She pulled a face, pushing up her nose and pulling down her lower eyelids.

I thought about how much I'd always longed for siblings and decided I didn't like Annie very much either. I remembered little Freddie with a pang and wondered how he was settling into his new family.

'Come on,' said Annie. 'Let's go and wash that muck off your face. Don't worry about Tom, he's just a big drip.' She paused. 'He likes you, though.'

I thought he had a funny way of showing it. It didn't matter much either way. But, walking back to the house and listening to Annie's chatter, I noticed again that she and her brother both had the most beautiful eyes, hazel-green and clear, with a fringe of long dark lashes.

Chapter Nine

I was miserable all through that dank, raw, muddy, chilly autumn, when it rained often and we were surrounded by a sea of mud. The Powell family were kind enough, mostly, though always occupied with something. On the second day, Mrs Powell asked me to call her Auntie Janet, it sounded friendlier, she said, and as though I was part of the family. I wasn't part of the family and she wasn't my aunt, so I said, politely, 'I'd rather not, thank you.'

Her weather-beaten face looked a little hurt, but she just said, 'Well, as you please, dear.'

So I went on calling her Mrs Powell and her husband Mr Powell.

I don't suppose they were really bothered much about what I called them. The two of them worked from early morning until darkness fell, mostly out of doors. Mr Powell struggled day after day to get his potato harvest in, grumbling at the wet weather that made the potatoes come up with lumps of mud sticking to them. Mrs Powell seemed to do everything else, feeding the livestock – the two milking cows, the pig, geese, ducks, chickens – doing the milking, driving the old truck to town on errands as well as feeding the family, making butter, preserving and bottling and pickling and making jam with the fruit and vegetables they grew themselves. There had been a good, fine summer this year, she said, until this dratted wet weather set in and didn't know when to stop. The girls and Tom had jobs of their own to do, both inside and out, and did them with varying degrees of enthusiasm. I was better fed than I had been for a long time, none of the rationing of cheese and butter and so many other things. Mrs Powell sometimes made bread, firing up the bread-oven built into the kitchen wall and using a long-handled shovel to put in the dough, which came out as wonderful-smelling crusty loaves.

But despite being well fed, I was still miserable. I hated the endless mud, the cackling geese that would nip your ankles if you weren't careful, the trips to the outhouse that needed boots and a torch if it was dark, plus a coat if it was raining.

I started school in the village about ten days after coming to the Powells', when half-term ended. Annie was a little younger than me, I was twelve already, but we were both in the same class, and also, I found, were Marjorie and a few others of the evacuees. We were drawn together like magnets when playtime came.

'What are yours like?' asked Marjorie. I knew at once she meant the billeting families.

I shrugged. 'They're all right. I don't like the farm much, though. It's muddy, and I have to work.'

The jobs I did were not too arduous, collecting eggs or carrying a pail of swill to the pigsty, as well as some indoor things. But I was beginning to feel put-upon. Marjorie gave me a sympathetic squeeze. We had never been particular friends before, but being evacuees seemed to create a new bond between us. She said, 'Poor you! Mine are nice. They live in this big house just up the road from here, plenty of room for the three of us girls. I even get a room to myself; the other two share. They're two ladies, one's a nurse and the other's a schoolteacher at the grammar school in the town and they've never been married because their sweethearts got killed in the last war. My room is lovely, and there's a proper bathroom. And they're going to get new dresses for all of us!'

Just her luck, I thought, Marjorie always seems to fall on her feet. One of the other girls, Mavis, said she didn't like the people she was with. Their children teased her and made fun of the way she talked. 'And it's them that talk funny, not me!' she said indignantly.

I was beginning to get used to the strange border accent, part Welsh lilt, part Herefordshire burr, or so I'd been told. They used some strange words that had puzzled me at first – *anunt* for 'opposite', *I warn* for 'I suppose', *ognel* for 'awkward' or 'contrary', *tush* for 'drag' and many others. Sometimes it seemed like a whole new language. But then they looked blankly at me or laughed if I said *apples and pears* for 'stairs' or *rabbit and pork* for 'talk' so I suppose we were in the same boat.

I wondered where Freddie was, and looked for him among the infants in the boys' part of the playground, but couldn't see him. I hoped he was all right. I knew nothing about him really; maybe he hadn't started school yet. The others began to vie with each other, either boasting about the great places they had or complaining about the way they were treated. I could see Annie hovering about, no doubt wondering what we were all saying. Some talked about being hungry all the time. I certainly couldn't complain about that, and reluctantly began to have the feeling that maybe I was not as badly off after all up at the farm.

And then they killed the pig.

That day stands out in my mind with terrible clarity, even all these decades afterwards. Annie told me what they were going to do that morning.

'What for?' I asked, horrified.

'To eat, of course.'

I stared at her in horror. 'You don't mean – you don't mean you kill old Percy and then you *eat* him?'

She laughed at my stricken face. 'Course we do. Where do you think all the bacon and ham and faggots come from?'

I felt sick. I didn't like Percy much, or the way he grunted and rooted about in the mud and squinted at me with his little piggy eyes when I took his food. But to kill him and then *eat* him – it would surely feel like being a cannibal to eat someone you knew and saw every day.

'It's not very nice,' admitted Annie. 'I can't bear hearing them squeal. I usually get into bed and keep my ears under the covers.'

I resolved to do the same. But when the dreadful process started, and there was a thin high squealing that went on and on, I could hear it even with my fingers in my ears and my head under the blankets.

Afterwards was even worse. The next day, on my way to collect eggs, I caught a glimpse of a huge, pale, dead body hanging head down from a beam in the big barn. I'd seen carcases in butchers' shops, of course, though I always tried to avert my eyes, but this was something else. And when I passed Percy's empty pen with the door ajar, I was almost sick there and then. I vowed I would never, ever eat bacon or ham again. And that I would pray that the war would end soon and I could go home to London.

But it didn't, and my misery grew. There were joints of fresh meat in the dairy, and faggot-making in the kitchen. But worst of all was the horrid task of stripping fat from a tin bath full of intestines, to be rendered down for lard. The whole house smelled of fat and raw meat, and for days I could not eat.

The year was heading towards Christmas and Mrs Powell was worried about me. I heard her and her husband talking in the kitchen one evening when I'd come down for a drink of water. The stairs had a bend in it, and opened into the kitchen. I stopped at the bend and paused, listening to the voices.

'I dread to think what she'll be like when we start on the Christmas poultry,' said Mrs Powell, who sounded as though she was peeling potatoes for next day, with a scraping sound and then a plop as she put them into cold water.

Mr Powell was a man of few words, and often fell asleep in his chair in the dark evenings. That, or his head was buried in a farming paper, or he was listening to the wireless for war news.

'She's hardly eating, and I swear she's losing weight,' continued Mrs Powell. 'Peaky ever since the pig killing. Too squeamish for her own good. Not a good match for us here.' She paused. 'Maybe she'd be better off somewhere else.'

I felt a strange pang at her words. Yes, I hated it here, but – would anywhere else be better? Mrs Powell was kind, and her husband too, in his way. Tom was a tease and Annie an inquisitive chatterer, and Sylvia constantly wished aloud to be somewhere else. But I'd grown used to them all. I wasn't sure I wanted to move…

I coughed to make myself heard and came down the stairs. Mrs Powell gave me a bright smile. 'Hello, dear. Fancy a snack, do you?'

I shook my head. 'Just a drink of water.'

'We were just talking about Christmas,' said Mrs Powell, which was a bit of a fib really but kindly meant. 'And I thought – I wonder if June would like it if we asked her ma down for a day or two?'

My heart leapt. 'Oh – could we?'

'Yes, why not? I'll drop her a line tomorrow.' And she came over and actually gave me a hug.

I looked forward to Christmas wholeheartedly from then on. Having Mum there would be wonderful. But it didn't happen. She had accepted Mrs Powell's invitation, but then, at the very last moment, my hopes were cruelly dashed. A letter came to say that she couldn't come after all. My dad had been slightly wounded, and after treatment would be coming home for a short leave to recover. He would not be fit to travel to the farm, and Mum felt that she must stay to take care of him.

Interlude

Juniper

I don't often cry, but I did on the way home from Nana's that first day. We had finished up at a sad point and I could see she was getting tired and didn't want to go on for now. Mom was home before me, still in her business suit and heels. Her keen eyes soon noticed my red ones.

'Are you OK, honey? Is Nana OK?'

I nodded. 'Yes, we're both good. We had a brilliant day, but we just got to a sad part of the story, I guess.'

I went to the fridge for a drink. Mom seemed concerned. 'Are you sure this storytelling is the best thing for you both? Wouldn't it be better if you played cards, or watched TV or did something relaxing?'

I shook my head decidedly. 'No! She wants to tell her story and I want to hear it. I expect it will be better tomorrow.' I took myself off to my bedroom and pulled out the notebook where I had scribbled notes as Nana had talked. I'd start to make some sense of what I'd written before I forgot. I opened my laptop.

'Juni!' called Mom. 'I'm getting a quick shower and then we're picking Dad up from work and going to dinner at Luigi's. Get yourself washed and tidied up.'

I sighed and closed the laptop. I could hardly wait for tomorrow to come.

Chapter Ten

June

It was sometime after Christmas that I decided I would run away. Christmas had been as festive as Mrs Powell could make it, but it had been preceded by a great and nauseating upheaval when geese, ducks and chickens were prepared for the Christmas market. I wanted to blot it out of my memory. The New Year had come in, raw, dank, chilly and grey, which matched my mood. I had been bitterly disappointed that my mum had not been able to come as she'd promised, although she'd sent gifts and a letter saying how sorry she was, and that my dad was progressing very nicely, considering.

Annie, with her inquisitive nose for secrets, suspected that I was up to something. I had begun making plans, hoarding bits of food that I could carry in a rucksack, trying to work out a route for getting back to London, which I was determined never to leave again, no matter how many bombs were falling. Annie wanted to know why I had a railway timetable under my pillow, that someone at school had managed to get for me. I studied it at night when Annie was asleep, with a torch under the bedclothes.

'Do you think you're going somewhere?'

'No, course not. Where would I go? I just got that because – because we're doing a composition on railways.'

She looked suspicious. 'I haven't heard about it.'

'No – well, it's extra. Miss Parry thinks I need to catch up on some things.'

I was telling lie upon lie. Miss Parry, I knew, was surprised at how good I was at almost all subjects by comparison with the others. Annie wasn't convinced. 'Well, I've never been on a train, so if you get the chance, take me along.' She sighed. 'But we've neither of us got the money.'

This was true. The Powells were kind, but they had little or no spare cash for children's pocket money. And a fare to London would cost a lot. I did have a carefully hoarded £5 note that my mother had given me before I left. I hoped that would be enough. I sighed, and stared out the window. The sky was leaden, overcast and full of something that didn't feel good.

'Dad says it's going to snow,' said Annie. 'And then we'll be proper stuck. We could be snowed in for weeks.'

I thought – and then I'll never get away. I can't stand to be stuck here for weeks and weeks more. I'll have to go soon. Tonight, even.

By bedtime, it was already beginning to snow, big, feathery flakes that floated like thistledown in the thin beam of a torch, settling on the muddy ground. Annie was excited as we prepared for bed.

'No school tomorrow, if it snows all night! We'll be able to go out and take a couple of trays up the Banky

Field for sledging. Dad and Mum hate snow because of the extra work. But I love it!'

My heart was beating fast as I lay awake waiting for her to begin her wiffly night-time snore. Everyone else went early to bed. Surely I could get to the station in the village, snow or no snow, before morning, and be on the early train. I climbed out of bed and dressed hurriedly, putting on my dungarees, an extra jersey, extra socks and my winter coat and woolly hat. I went to the wardrobe and got my canvas knapsack, an old one of Tom's which he'd said I could have. I'd stuffed it with food, a tin of corned beef, a couple of spam sandwiches saved from tea, half a loaf, and a couple of Mrs Powell's rock cakes from a couple of days ago, which would be truly rock-like by now. I also had a torch, the railway timetable and an old lemonade bottle filled with water. I tiptoed downstairs into the silent kitchen with the range still glowing, the cats snoozing and the clock tick-tocking loudly on the wall. I found my Wellington boots, pulled on my woolly gloves and let myself out by the back door.

The cold hit me at once and made me gasp; the big feathery flakes had turned into small sharp stinging ones and the wind had risen. Already the snow was beginning to drift, some of the yard had places scoured bare, while there were small drifts piling up against the walls of the house and buildings. I had a moment of indecision, thinking of the warm feather bed I had left, and the long trudge into the village. But I shouldered my knapsack and set off.

I did not know how long it would take me to reach the village on foot, and suddenly thought it might be a long wait until seven in the morning when the first train ran. With luck the family would not discover my absence until I was safely on the way to London. And if I was early, I could wait in the nice warm waiting room where I guessed there would be a coal fire.

It was hard to stand upright with the snow and wind driving into my face. Bent almost double, I struggled along between the bare branches of the hazels and hawthorns that edged the farm track, switching on the thin beam of the torch to light me when I stumbled against a rut. It seemed to take an age to reach the first corner, where the farm track came out into the narrow road to the village. I saw the bulk of the shed at the end of the track where Mr Powell's fertiliser and other things were delivered to save the vans tackling the rutted track. I was breathless and my hands already felt numb, despite my woolly gloves. I decided I would rest for a moment in the shelter of the building before taking the village road.

It felt warmer inside, away from the wind and stinging snow. There were some piles of hay and straw there as well as the fertiliser sacks. I took off the knapsack and my gloves, and tucked my hands inside my coat to warm them. The hay smelled fragrant and inviting. I sat down and burrowed into it, pulling more over me. I'd rest for a little; it must be past midnight by now and I was tired. The wind whistled through the cracks and I could hear the snow splattering against the walls. My eyes closed.

I was awakened suddenly by voices and lights, then hands touching me. I'd been dreaming of my bed at home, peaceful and quiet with no sirens and no bombs.

Someone said, 'She's here!' and the light was shining into my eyes as I opened them.

'Is she dead?' I recognised that voice as Tom's, excited and curious but somehow anxious too. And then his father replying, 'No, no, just fast asleep. Now then, lass, what's all this, then?' And they were pulling me to my feet and brushing the hay off. Mr Powell did not wait for an answer, but went on, 'She'll be half-starved with cold. Tom, you run back quick as you can and tell Mother she's found, and to poke up the fire and get summat hot, like soup, to warm her up.'

And without more ado, he picked me up like a baby and carried me out of the shed, kicking the door shut behind him. Tom ran ahead through the whirling snowflakes, the torch bobbing as he slipped and slithered along.

I half-dozed again, being carried bumpily along in the dark, with Mr Powell huffing and puffing, and every so often setting me on my feet for a while for him to get his breath. He didn't let go of me, though, held onto me all the time and then picked me up again. I felt embarrassed at being carried, and disappointed that my plan had failed, and cross with myself for falling asleep, and a whole lot of other things, but also, strangely, a feeling of relief. Between puffing and blowing, Mr Powell told me that Annie had woken, found my bed cold and empty, and raised the alarm.

I felt sure that a whole heap of trouble would be waiting me back at the farm, sooner or later. We got back to find the whole household awake, Mrs Powell and the girls all exclaiming with relief when we appeared. Mrs

Powell shooed the three children off to bed again, saying that questions would have to wait, and Mr Powell pulled off his boots and followed soon after. Mrs Powell removed my damp outer clothes, wrapped me in a blanket and brought me hot Bovril and toast. She had stirred up the fire to a cheerful blaze. I felt my shivering gradually subside and my cold hands and feet begin to thaw. Mrs Powell fetched more blankets. 'I think you'd be better off down here in the warm for tonight,' she said. 'I'll tuck you up nice and cosy on the sofa, and I'll stop here in the armchair, just in case you take a fever or summat.'

I felt ashamed. I had caused them a great deal of trouble and they hadn't once been angry with me.

But Mrs Powell looked a little sad as she tucked the blankets round me.

'Is it so bad being here with us, then, that you want to run away?'

I felt my eyes fill with tears. 'No, you're kind to me. I just wanted to see my mum. And it's so dark here, and no houses about, and all the mud...' I stopped, not able to go on, and burst into tears. 'I'm sorry.'

Mrs Powell pulled up her husband's old armchair close to the sofa and stroked my hair. 'I understand, my love. It's all new and different to what you're used to. I daresay we would find it just as strange in a town. We should have spent more time making you feel at home, but there's always so much to do – maybe you'd have been better with someone else, someone in the village...'

The thought of being sent away made me weep afresh. In spite of everything, I suddenly knew without doubt that I wanted to stay. I said wretchedly, 'I'm sorry. I do want to stay here…'

'Well, let's forget about it, then, shall we, and start again? I'll try to spend a bit more time indoors with you, explaining things and that. It's a miserable old time of year on a farm, never mind with a war on as well, messing up everyone's lives.' She paused, her ruddy face thoughtful in the firelight. 'I hope as it'll soon be over and then you'll be back with your mum. But if not – if not, things won't stay like this for ever, you know. Winter is always the worst time. But spring comes, and summer – you wait! You wait until the birds start singing, when the buds start swelling and the sap rises up and the green comes back. You wait until it's the green time again.'

Chapter Eleven

Snow fell for several days, on and off, and sometimes it drifted, piling against the buildings and walls. At night there were hard frosts. When the snow stopped and a weak sun appeared in a wintry-blue sky, the snow on the roof melted by day and froze again, and a fringe of icicles hung from the eaves of the farmhouse.

The view was transformed and I was enchanted. Every field, every hill, every ugly farm building, large or small, even the midden by the cowsheds, was covered with a layer of pristine white, white so pure and clean that it made the whitewashed dairy look grubby by comparison. Each tree branch, twig and stem had its own covering, even the gateposts each had their round little caps of snow. I had never seen anything like this back in London, where any snow that fell was soon turned to grey slush in the streets.

True to her word, Annie begged tin trays from her mother, and she, Tom and I plodded through the snow to the top of the steep field behind the farm and sledged down it. I loved the feel of cold air buffeting my cheeks as I whizzed down, the swift rush and slight thrill of danger, wondering if we would stop at the bottom of the slope or carry on and crash into a fence or a tree. We would return carrying the trays, a little more battered and dented than before, our cheeks glowing with cold, our gloves soaked through and sometimes our socks as well if snow had got into our boots. Mrs Powell (or Auntie Janet as I now called her, since my attempt to run away) grumbled a little at the number of socks and gloves drying on the fireguard, but I could see that she was pleased and relieved that I had found something that I enjoyed. The snow made extra work for everyone, and soon turned dirty and brown as people and animals traipsed back and forth in the yard, and there was great effort involved when waterpipes froze. Nobody could get away from or come to the farm; we were well and truly snowed up. No danger of school. Sylvia hated it and fretted for a thaw and release. But to me it was a magical time, and I was sorry when a thaw did set in: water dripped, snow dissolved and patches of the same old greenish-brown fields and muddy yard began to show again.

February was dreary, wet and cold, but somehow there was a different feel to how it had been in November. Slowly, slowly, the days were lengthening, the dark evenings shorter, a feeling of better times ahead. And one day, Auntie Janet asked me to go to the orchard with her and showed me a wonderful sight. Beneath the still-bare apple and plum trees, a carpet of green spiky leaves with nodding white flowers, bell-shaped and delicately veined with green, stretched away under the trees. The sight was so beautiful it almost took my breath. 'What are they?'

'Snowdrops,' said Auntie Janet. 'February Fair Maids, they call them. I always love it when they come! They're the first sign that spring is not so far away. Don't tell me you've never seen them before?'

I had to admit I never had. They were so beautiful, so pure, so full of promise. And Auntie Janet had been right in her predictions. Before they had faded, more green spikes were pushing up, which before long budded and burst into golden daffodils, white narcissi, blue grape hyacinth. Auntie Janet told me she had planted the bulbs herself, hundreds of them, when she'd first come to the farm as a young bride, and like me, had hated the mud and dreariness of the first autumn and winter.

'There'll be tulips later,' she said. 'But you wait – wait until you see the first wildflowers!'

I was not disappointed when they came. First the delicate white wood anemones, shiny lacquered celandines, tiny blue violets thrusting up in the grass. Then the first primroses, buttercups, cowslips and many, many others that I did not have names for.

As spring came in, so the mood of the whole household changed. The dogged endurance of the winter months was replaced by a feeling of looking forward, of planning and preparing. Potato planting for this year's crops would be the next big job, when the ground was dry enough. News had come from the War Ag, as usual not welcomed by Mr Powell. 'They want us to put in another ten acres of spuds,' he grumbled at dinnertime on a chilly day in March, when a brisk wind rattled the bare wisteria stems against the farmhouse wall. An official-looking buff envelope had arrived by post that morning, delivered by the elderly postman on his bicycle.

Auntie Janet paused, a ladle in her hand for doling out rabbit stew from the big pot. 'How are we to do that? We don't have a spare ten acres to grow them.'

'They've got an answer to that,' said Mr Powell, 'There's the Boggy Field – not used for much now the sheep have all gone and all but the two milking cows.' His face grew sad and resentful, as it always did when he thought of his lost livestock.

'But it's got those wet boggy places! It can't be ploughed, never has been.'

'They've got an answer to that as well, interfering know-alls! They say it can be drained. They'll send a work team.'

'But there are no workers. Do they mean Land Girls?'

'No, not Land Girls. Prisoners of war.'

A little ripple of excitement and apprehension seemed to go round the table.

'Italians?' guessed Auntie Janet. Suddenly we were all listening.

He shook his head. 'No, none around here. These are Germans.'

'Oh boy – Germans!' Tom's eyes were gleaming.

Sylvia gave a little shriek and clasped her hands to her mouth. Her mother had gone a little paler than her usual ruddy look. 'Bill – surely not! There aren't any hereabouts.'

'Ah, but there are, Mother. Not too far away, there's that camp at Kingsbridge, not fifteen miles from here as the crow flies. Remember there was a big stink about it when they set it up? All gone quiet now. But those men are still there, and they're hiring them out to farmers.'

Auntie Janet sat down suddenly. 'Well, I don't know what to think! Germans here! Will we be safe?'

'Safe as houses, Mother. They'll have guards with them. And dogs, I daresay. And we may as well get some use of them while they're here. There's that fodder hut at the bottom corner, don't need it now the stock are gone. They can go in there to shelter if need be and have their dinner and that. They'll be fetched and taken back every day. Mind you, some places are billeting them on the farms…'

But this was a step too far for Auntie Janet. 'Well, that won't be happening here! I couldn't be doing with it, not with children about. I daresay they're safe enough, but let them keep their distance, I say.'

'Can I go and watch them?' asked Tom eagerly. 'Some might speak English! I'd like to know what guns they had in the war, and how they got captured and all sorts of things. Can I?'

'Indeed you cannot!' said his mother firmly, and gave him a rap on the knuckles with the ladle for good measure. 'Fraternising with the enemy, they call that. People get shot for it, I shouldn't wonder!'

'But we could just see them from a distance, couldn't we?' pleaded Annie. 'Just to see what they look like? I bet nobody at school has seen a real German!'

Sylvia shuddered. 'I don't want to see them! If one spoke to me, I'd just die, I know I would!' She tucked a strand of her blonde hair into place. Despite her words, I had the feeling she'd be quite interested to see a German POW herself.

I was silent, digesting this piece of news. Germans, here. Germans, who my dad had got wounded fighting against, who had bombed us mercilessly night after night, who were the cause of this dreadful war. They must be awful people. I did not want to see them and I hoped they wouldn't be here long.

Chapter Twelve

A few days later the workforce was there, arriving in an army vehicle and climbing out over the tailgate, a steady stream of men in mud-coloured clothes. Two guards with guns watched them, and walked alongside as they marched across our yard and through the gate that would lead them to the cow pasture and then to the Boggy Field. We children clustered round the window, scolded by Auntie Janet but unable to restrain our curiosity. What we expected I don't know, but what we saw was a couple of lines of ordinary men, some with sullen expressions, others more cheerful and looking about them with curiosity, all wearing the same clothing and the same heavy boots.

'They look just like ordinary men,' said Tom, sounding disappointed. 'I thought at least they'd have swastikas and things, and helmets.'

'For goodness' sake, come away from the window,' urged his mother. 'They're just men. Nothing to see.'

Sylvia shuddered in a dramatic way. 'They might look ordinary but they must be dreadful people. Think of what you hear in those news reports on the wireless.'

'I think you're better off not listening to that stuff,' snapped her mother. 'Fills your head with foolish fancies. Come on and get ready for school, all of you.'

The prisoners were still there when we got home from school, we could see them across the fields as we walked down the lane, mud-coloured men toiling with picks and shovels in a mud-coloured field. The guards stood to one side, guns across their arms. If a prisoner tried to make a break for it, I knew that shots would be fired. Tom echoed my thoughts. 'How far do you think they'd get if they tried to escape?' he wondered. 'They could get some of them to make a distraction, and then the others could overpower those guards, couldn't they?'

'You read too many comics,' said Annie, and gave him a shove.

After a few days, we got used to the men arriving every morning, working through the day and going off again in the evening. Some arrangement must have been made with Mr Powell, because every morning one of the guards would turn up, holding an empty billy-can which one of us would fill with milk for the men's tea. Both the guards seemed quite surly fellows; maybe it was a dull job keeping an eye on prisoners of war all day. They spoke with different accents; perhaps they were just fed up with the bleak countryside and wanted to go home. After a few rebuffs, Tom gave up the idea of plying them with questions.

Then one morning we had a shock. There was a shuffling at the back door which meant the guard had come to collect the milk. Sylvia went to open the door and we all heard her scream. She came back to the kitchen as white as a ghost, still holding the big enamel jug of milk, slopping its contents onto the stone flags. 'It's – it's one of *them*!'

Auntie Janet took the jug and marched to the door, the three of us following to see what the fuss was about. There stood, not the guard, but a young man in the mud-coloured overalls of the prisoners, holding the billy-can and smiling in a nervous kind of way. He had fair hair with a wave in it, his eyes were very blue and he looked hardly more than a boy. He said, 'Please, I come for the milk.'

Auntie Janet had been slightly flustered, but soon regained her composure. 'Oh – I see. It's usually – someone else.'

The young man nodded and smiled. '*Ja*. Yes. Today he is…' He rubbed his stomach and bent over with a grimace of pain.

'Oh, I see, he's poorly.' Auntie Janet took the can from him and filled it from the jug. The prisoner looked beyond her at our three inquisitive young faces peering at him. 'Ah – good day, children. I am pleased to meet you. My name is Conrad.'

We looked at each other, not knowing how to react. What should you say to an enemy? 'Don't tell your names,' hissed Tom. He stepped forward and said boldly, 'I am Robert. This is Margaret and – er – Doris, and my other sister is Susan.'

Auntie Janet rounded on him. 'Don't be so silly! Your name is Tom and the girls are Annie and June.' She turned back to the young man. 'I'm afraid they read too many silly comic books.'

The young man actually threw back his head and laughed. 'I have young brothers and a sister myself, back home.' At the mention of home, the laughter left his eyes. 'I miss them.'

'I'm sure you do,' said Auntie Janet. 'The sooner this dreadful war is over, the better.'

'Amen to that. *Danke schön* – thank you so much.' He picked up the billy-can and was gone.

Auntie Janet turned back to us, very annoyed. 'What is the matter with you children? Whispering and telling downright lies! Where are your manners?'

Tom protested. 'Mum, he's the *enemy*! You shouldn't give out info, that's why they cover up the road signs and turn signposts around! And now he knows our names. Goodness knows what will happen…'

'I can tell you what will happen, you're not too old to get your backside warmed, young man! I never heard such nonsense! That was just a young lad, not much older than our Sylvia by the looks of him, a prisoner in a strange country and far away from home. If you can't be civil and polite, then I'm ashamed of you!'

I had never heard Auntie Janet so cross. The unexpected visit of the young German had thrown us all off balance. Sylvia came out from behind the dairy door where she had been listening, and got the sharp edge of her mother's tongue too. 'As for you, Miss, screaming and carrying on – well! That young man's manners could teach you all something!'

She went into the dairy and began a clattering of milk buckets and then the whirring of the cream separator. We looked at each other. 'Well,' said Tom in his own defence, 'it was her who told us we shouldn't fraternise with the enemy.'

Annie seemed uncertain. 'He didn't seem like an enemy. Just like an ordinary person, really. He looked homesick when he talked about his family.'

I could sympathise with that. It was quite a novel idea, that German prisoners of war might be longing to go home to their families, not just wanting to kill us and drop bombs.

'He was really quite nice-looking,' said Sylvia thoughtfully.

Auntie Janet's face appeared from the dairy door, still cross. 'When you've all finished standing round gossiping, maybe you'll get on with your Saturday jobs. Tom, come and turn the handle of this separator. Sylvia, get some kettles boiling. I'm going to make butter today. You two girls go and change your beds and tidy your room – it's like a pigsty in there.'

We scattered to our tasks. But we were all strangely disturbed by the visit of the young prisoner. Annie was inclined to giggle as we struggled with changing the sheets on our beds, flapping them about and calling me Doris. The incident had made me thoughtful, and I found that I couldn't get the young man out of my mind, and hoped that we would see him again.

Chapter Thirteen

We did see Conrad again, many times. What happened to the sick guard I don't know, but after that morning it was almost always Conrad who came to get the milk.

'Must be a "trusty",' said Mr Powell.

Auntie Janet grew quite attached to the young man, feeling sorry for him being so far away from his own mother, and taking him under her wing.

'If ever you were in his position, which heaven forbid,' she told Tom sternly, 'I'd like to think that some good person would take pity on you and show you what kindness they could.'

All of us got used to seeing him about, and we grew to like him. In the few brief minutes he was allowed, he loved to talk about his young brothers and sister, Wolfgang, Heinrich and Helga. Helga was mine and Annie's age, and had long blonde hair she wore in plaits, like me. Wolfgang and Heinrich were, he said, 'naughty monkeys' who liked to play tricks on people. He had not seen them since the war began and did not know when he would see them again. That made him sad. Tom wanted to talk about the fighting, but Conrad did not want to.

Usually when Tom started his questions, Conrad would pick up the billy-can and say he had to go.

The days were lengthening and the two milking cows had been put out to pasture by day now that there was new grass, though they still came in overnight. Nobody else wanted the routine task of taking the cows, Tulip and Marigold, to pasture in the morning and bringing them in for milking in the afternoon, so the task soon fell to me. I had lost all fear of them and quite enjoyed ambling leisurely along with them. They were never in any great hurry either way and, as the grass grew, had the habit of snatching mouthfuls from beneath the hedgerows as they went. As March merged into April, the piercing wind softened, and the mud was beginning to dry out.

One morning as we wandered our way to the pasture, I saw the figure of Conrad coming from the Boggy Field, carrying the empty billy-can. He was later than usual this morning. He opened the gate for me to drive the cows through.

'*Guten morgen, fräulein* June – or is it Doris?' he said with a twinkle in his blue eyes. 'A beautiful morning, is it not?'

I gave Marigold a slap on her bony rump to hurry her along and closed the gate behind her. Conrad was waiting. I would have to walk back to the farm with him. A few weeks ago the prospect would have filled me with terror, but now it did not. It was a very pleasant morning, with a twittering of birds in the hedgerows and white clouds scurrying across a blue sky. Conrad did not seem in a hurry to return to work.

I agreed that it was a beautiful day, and that my name was definitely not Doris.

'June, then.' His accent meant that he pronounced a J with a 'Ch' sound, which came out as 'Choon'. I smiled.

'Well, Choon, is it school for you today?'

I nodded and pulled a face. It was strange, but I was beginning to enjoy the rhythms of farm life, the milking and feeding of the animals, even the hard jobs like cleaning their pens. From the farmyard I heard the cackling of the geese as they were let out, and could see the line of ducks waddling in single file to the duck pond. I wished I did not have to go to school today.

Conrad sighed. 'You know, I come from a farm too. I did not appreciate it at the time, was keen to join the army and see life. But now I cannot wait to return.'

'You speak very good English,' I said, and went red, feeling I had been too forward.

'I learned in school, and more since I was captured.'

We were coming to the farmyard. I saw Sylvia at the window, looking both surprised and annoyed to see us walking along together. She flung open the door before we reached it. 'June, you're going to be late for school. Hurry up and get your coat and shoes on.'

She snatched the billy-can from Conrad and sloshed the milk into it.

'Sylvia's in a bad mood,' I said to Annie as we got our school mackintoshes from the pegs behind the door.

Annie grinned. 'She was mad that you walked back with Conrad. She's a bit sweet on him, haven't you noticed?'

Now that she mentioned it, I realised that Sylvia did seem to be the one most often getting the milk these days, and I also remembered that she'd been doing her hair in a different way lately, that made her look older. Also that she'd taken to dolling herself up in different things, adding a little scarf or a belt. I'd thought she was trying to look like a film star, but maybe she was trying to impress Conrad.

'Dad is peeved about it,' said Annie, fastening the buckle on her mac. 'Mum likes Conrad, but I don't think she'd like it either if her daughter fell in love with a German.'

'He's nice, though,' I said, and then had to turn my head away because I was blushing again.

After that, it often seemed to work out that I was turning out the cows when Conrad was coming for the milk and we walked home together, which didn't please Sylvia one little bit.

'I think your sister is flirting with me a little,' he remarked one morning. 'She is a very pretty girl, but I am really not interested. If I marry, I will choose a nice German girl, I think.'

I felt the tiniest bit annoyed on Sylvia's behalf, and I also had to put him straight on something. 'Sylvia is very pretty and she likes you a lot,' I said. 'But she is not my sister.' I paused. 'I'm from London really. I'm an evacuee.'

Conrad stopped and looked at me, as though light had suddenly dawned. 'Ah. Then that is why your speech is different. I wondered.' He began to walk again. 'Do you miss home?'

I felt a lump rise in my throat and tears come to my eyes. I blinked them away. I was getting to like the farm now, and in any case, I mustn't show myself to be a cry-baby. But I still missed home dreadfully.

'Yes,' I said, and my voice came out as a hoarse whisper.

He did not look at me or comment for a moment, then he said gently, 'You and I, then, we are the same. Both exiles, both homesick.'

And then the tears spilled over and I felt them hot on my cheeks, and brushed them away angrily, reminding myself that after all, Conrad was the enemy and I shouldn't show weakness in front of him. He did not embarrass me by showing he'd noticed, but after a while he said thoughtfully, 'In a way, Choon, it must be harder for you. I joined the army voluntarily, you were forced to leave home. You are only a child. War is hard on children.'

I gulped and nodded. 'It's horrible.'

He was quiet for a while. We had almost reached the farmhouse. Then he said, 'Now spring is here, it will be better. For everyone. It always is. You'll see, Choon, now the birds are building, now the sun shines – sometimes – now the grass is growing and trees budding and it's green again, it will all seem better.' We had reached the back door. He gestured with his free hand towards the yard gate. 'Look! That tree, a hawthorn, I think. You see? Already the green comes!'

I looked at the hawthorn, which all winter had stood bare and lifeless, it's branches stark and black against a grey winter sky. Now, following his pointing finger, I saw that tiny buds were beginning to break out, unfurling all along every twig and cloaking the branches in a haze of tender new green.

Chapter Fourteen

Once spring had decided it was really on its way, there
was no holding it back. Suddenly, the quiet, grey, dull
landscape had colour and movement and activity. Auntie
Janet's sitting hen, which I had watched become 'broody'
some weeks ago, clucking and fussing and tucking her
own eggs and those belonging to others away underneath
her, suddenly became the mother of a dozen yellow,
cheeping balls of fluff. They hatched one at a time, first a
small hole appearing in an egg, followed by a tiny beak
that busily pecked away at the surrounding eggshell
until, with a mighty heave and a splintering of the shell,
the small, bedraggled chick was born into the world.
Within a few minutes they would dry out to become
enchanting fluffy balls, inquisitive and eager to explore
the big new world. One of the geese hatched goslings,
and announced their arrival with a great cackling and
fussing and clapping of wings. We were warned to keep
clear of geese with goslings, especially of the gander, who
became fiercely protective when he had young offspring
and would hiss and peck at anyone venturing too near.
The goslings were very sweet too, little greeny-yellow
creatures who soon learned to stretch their necks and flap

their tiny wings in imitation of their elders. A couple of ducks also proudly produced miniature versions of themselves, and encouraged them to waddle off to the nearest water almost as soon as they hatched.

The family mourned the fact that they no longer saw baby lambs in the fields in springtime. 'The War Ag took all our sheep,' said Annie sadly.

I'd heard a lot of talk about the War Ag and was puzzled. 'What is the War Ag?'

'War Agricultural Executive Committee,' said Annie, and pulled a face. 'They've got powers to make farmers do what they want. Like take the sheep and grow potatoes instead. I used to help with the lambing, you know, when there was a difficult birth. Sometimes the lambs don't come out head-first like they're supposed to. The heads have to be turned. Dad said I was the best one for that, 'cos my hands are the smallest to get in and turn the head round. And then grab the front legs and pull the lamb out. I think I might be a vet when I'm older.'

I felt this was a bit too much information for me to stomach, but I admired Annie for being able to do such a thing. Marigold had a new calf, and Annie said that it would soon be taken too, most likely.

And the green time had come, as Auntie Janet and Conrad had promised. Every time you looked there seemed to be more tiny buds unfurling on the oak and ash and sycamores, buds which unfolded into leaves of fresh green. Auntie Janet's forsythia shrub had bloomed into a glory of bright yellow flowers early on, even before the leaves came, like a burst of sunshine beside the back door. There was another shrub with pink buds, that

Auntie Janet said was a flowering currant. There were red tulips as she had promised. But mostly it was the green that enchanted me. I had never imagined anything so beautiful.

And the draining of the Boggy Field was finished. It was ready to be ploughed and planted with potatoes for the feeding of the British people.

'We'll all have to help with the planting,' said Auntie Janet, and Tom and Annie groaned.

Conrad came to say goodbye, a very quick visit because the truck was coming to pick them up for the very last time. This time he had no billy-can, but instead he carried a posy of wildflowers, pale yellow primroses and tiny wild violets he had found under a hedgerow. He presented them to Auntie Janet with a little bow and a clicking of his heels in the big boots. I could see that she was very touched. 'I think it is your Mothering Sunday very soon,' he said. 'I want to thank you for your kindness, Mrs Chanet, for treating me like a son.'

Auntie Janet's face was a picture. She did not often receive flowers, or compliments, and I would have bet my life that none of her children had remembered that it was Mothering Sunday soon. I'd forgotten about it myself.

She said, 'Oh, thank you. Thank you so much, Conrad,' and covered her confusion by going to find a little glass to put the flowers in. Conrad shook hands with each of us in turn, solemnly wishing us everything good for the future. He assured us that when the war was over, he would come and visit us again. Tom could not resist saying, boldly, 'When we've won the war, you mean.'

I wanted to kick Tom, but Conrad only smiled a little sadly. 'We shall see.'

I was sad that there would be no more morning walks from the cow pasture with Conrad, with him telling me the names, in English and German, of the nesting birds and of the wildflowers springing up along the verges. There were tears in my eyes again as he squeezed my hand, and said, 'Be happy, Choon.' I was surprised that Sylvia was not more upset to see the last of Conrad. Not that her efforts at flirtation had met with much response, but that hadn't stopped her trying. She just shook his hand like the rest of us and said very casually, 'Well, so long Conrad, all the best.'

I discovered the reason for that soon afterwards, when the army truck and its passengers had pulled out of the yard and disappeared down the track and I was trying to hide my sadness. Sylvia had cycled into the village to see her friend Helen the evening before, and seemed bursting with some news. 'You'll never guess! There's going to be an American base at Wayland Hall, just down the road! Isn't it fantastic? Helen says they bring all kinds of things with them to give out, and they like our village because it's quaint, and they put on all kinds of things like parties and dances and picture shows! Maybe we'll get invited!'

Auntie Janet looked very dubious. 'Well, I don't know about that, Sylvia. You never know what they'll be like. Americans are not like us. And parties, dances – you're only fifteen, you know.'

'Almost sixteen!' said Sylvia indignantly. 'Helen's parents will let her go, I know. Oh please, Mum, don't be mean! I might even meet someone who knows people in Hollywood!'

I thought wryly that it hadn't taken much to get her mind off Conrad.

'Sylvia, calm down,' said her mother. 'They're not even here yet. You haven't been invited to anything. And I don't know what your father's going to say.'

For a usually quiet man, Mr Powell had quite a lot to say when he heard this piece of news. 'Bloomin' Yanks, coming here flashing their money and showing off, thinking they're going to win the war for us, just like they did in the last lot. Hope they keep theirselves to theirselves, that's all.'

Sylvia didn't say anything, but I saw her lips set in a stubborn line. And later in the week, she brought home a dress that Helen's mum had passed on to her, old-fashioned but very pretty with a pattern of pink rosebuds on a cream background, and began to cut it up and fuss with paper patterns to make a new dress for herself. The picture on the pattern looked pretty too, short puffed sleeves, a tiny waist and what Sylvia called a 'sweetheart neckline'. I knew she was planning ahead for the possibility of being invited to a party at the American base, whatever her father said.

There seemed to be a big hole in my life now that the prisoners of war had left us. My thoughts were turning back to my mum and dad. I'd had two or three letters from Mum since Christmas, one saying that my dad was making good progress, another saying that he had returned to active service. That gave me a shock. 'It isn't fair!' I burst out when I read the letter. 'He's been wounded once, he shouldn't have to go back!' The tears never seemed very far away these days.

'It's what happens, my love,' said Auntie Janet. 'Patch them up and send them back, that's what they do, I'm afraid.' Seeing my woebegone face, she went on kindly, 'Besides, he wouldn't want to sit round twiddling his thumbs now he's well again, I don't suppose. Don't you fret, my lovely. I've just had an idea. With Mothering Sunday coming up soon, how would you like it if I was to ask your mum to come down for a day or two? Annie could go in with Sylvia, she could share with you. Would you like that? If she can manage it, of course. I'll write this evening if you like.'

She was as good as her word. Mum's letter came back almost by return of post. Yes, she could make it. She was owed time off from work. She was missing June so much. It was very kind of Mrs Powell to ask. She'd love to come.

Interlude
Juniper

I gave Mom a big hug when we saw each other that evening. She seemed surprised. We didn't usually do a lot of hugging. 'What was that for?'

I said, 'Because I love you and I'd hate it if you weren't here.'

'I'm not going anywhere, honey,' said Mom. 'And I love you too. How was Nana today?'

'She didn't see her mom for ages in the war, and she missed her dreadfully,' I said. 'But she's seeing her soon, in the story. I can't wait to hear about it.'

Chapter Fifteen

June

Mum looked the same but different somehow, the same person but thinner, older and smaller. Auntie Janet had brought me in the old truck to meet her at the station. We saw her before she saw us, getting off the train clutching her battered old suitcase and looking about her. I started to wave frantically. My shouts of 'Mum! Mum!' couldn't be heard above the hissing and steaming of the train, but then she saw me, her face lit up, and she became my old Mum again. I raced down the platform and flung myself into her arms. She hugged me back and then held me away from her and said, 'This big girl can't be my June, surely!'

I wasn't aware that I had grown, although I had noticed that my school clothes seemed to be getting a bit shorter and tighter. I laughed and said, 'It *is* me, Mum!' and she laughed too. Auntie Janet came up and there were introductions all round. Mum and Auntie Janet seemed a little awkward with each other to begin with. Both of them seemed to be trying to talk a bit more like what my teacher called the 'King's English', with comical results as Auntie Janet had the local border Welsh accent and Mum was pure Cockney. But they'd forgotten all that by the time we reached the farm and were chattering away like old friends.

The days with Mum flew past. The Powell family liked her, and she did her best to fit in, helping with washing-up and preparing meals. Sylvia questioned her endlessly about London and the films showing in the West End, and the Windmill theatre which had stayed open throughout the Blitz and never closed its doors. She couldn't understand it when Mum said, 'I've never been to the Windmill, I've hardly ever been up West, to be honest, even before the war.' Tom wanted to know about the Blitz, and the German bombers, and what it felt like when the bombs were falling, and what barrage balloons were like, and he was disappointed when Mum wasn't all that keen to talk about it.

Mum and I talked long into the night, she in Annie's bed and I in mine. She wanted to know about everything, what the school was like, and the teachers, and the other children, especially my fellow evacuees. 'How is Marjorie? Are you two still good friends?'

Marjorie and I hadn't been particularly good friends before, and things weren't any different now. There were girls that I liked and girls I didn't much, same as back home. Some of the locals were sneery about the evacuees, laughed at the way we talked and called us names. I didn't tell Mum, though. I'd got used to it. Besides, Annie usually stuck up for me and sometimes Tom too, although he was at the grammar school with Sylvia.

'And what about that little lad who you were given charge of for the journey?' asked Mum. 'Freddie, was it?

Poor little feller, he looked like he'd been neglected. His mum was killed, you know, the teacher told me, and he didn't have a dad. Did he settle all right?'

'I don't know,' I said. Freddie hadn't come to our school, and I hadn't seen him about the village. I thought about him sometimes and hoped he was happy with his host family. But what had actually happened to him remained a mystery.

Mum couldn't get used to Auntie Janet's driving, and clutched the sides of the seat whenever we went anywhere in the truck.

'I can't get my head round the idea of women driving,' she told me privately when we were alone in our bedroom. 'It don't seem right somehow. I mean, I know there are women driving ambulances and all sorts in London, even Princess Elizabeth drives one, but that's because of the war. Catch me ever driving a car! I'll stick to the buses, thank you all the same. And I must say Mrs Powell is a bit – what you might call erratic. Although she's very nice,' she added hurriedly, I suppose in case I thought she might be criticising Auntie Janet. I agreed that Auntie Janet's driving could be a little scary.

I showed Mum round the farmyard and the fields, pointing out the things I thought might interest her. She tried hard to be interested, but could not get over her anxieties about the countryside.

'It's so – empty,' she said, as we leaned together on the cow pasture gate. 'There's nothing but fields. And trees, and more fields, and hills. No houses anywhere, except another farm here and there with half a mile between. Makes me nervous.'

I had felt the same at first, and I understood. The absence of houses and streets and *people* had seemed frightening to me too. But I was beginning to love the space and the freedom, the room to breathe.

'I like it,' I said.

'Well, I'm glad of that,' said Mum. 'At least it's a comfort to us, your dad and me, to know you're in a place where it's safe and quiet, and where people are good to you. I don't think I could stick it long, though. There are a lot of *creatures* about, aren't there? Spiders and earwigs in the house, and I'm sure I saw a mouse running across the kitchen floor, and those bats that fly about at night give me the willies. Aren't you scared they'll get in your hair? And don't ask me to go anywhere near those vicious geese! And the cows – oh, there's one coming now; quick, get back from the gate!'

Tulip was ambling along the hedgerow, snatching at the tall grass that was beginning to line the ditch, not at all interested in anything else. I laughed at Mum's list of woes and fears. She would always be a townie, while I was beginning to see myself as a country girl. Then she began to talk about Dad, which made me sad. And I cried when it was time to see her off again for home on the London train. She was trying hard to be brave, biting her lip and forcing herself to smile. 'I'll come and see you again soon, love, when I can get the time off. It's been ever so nice being here. You keep on eating all that butter and cream and I'll hardly know you next time I come.' She turned away, I guessed so I would not see her tears, and climbed aboard, clutching her suitcase, into which Auntie Janet had pressed some farm goodies, a piece of cheese, a few well-wrapped eggs, a pot of gooseberry jam. When she waved from the window as the train pulled out, she had a smile on her face, and I knew she would keep it in place until she was out of sight.

I felt my own control begin to wobble, and although I struggled to hold it back, a sob escaped me as we were walking back to the truck. Auntie Janet heard. She stopped and took my hand. 'Don't cry, my lovely. The time will pass quickly, you'll see. I know, why don't we stop by May's shop in the village and see what she's got in the way of sweets? They might even have some chocolate creams. I've got my ration book.'

May's shop doorbell tinkled as we went in. May was a stout woman who kept a bit of everything: candles, vegetables, tools, paraffin, pots and pans, matches, cough remedies and whatever other items she could get hold of. Sometimes the sweetie jars behind the counter held bullseyes or toffees or jelly babies, sometimes there wasn't much on offer. She shook her head apologetically when Auntie Janet asked for chocolate.

'Sorry, Janet. All out. We do have some boiled sweets and liquorice.'

There were a few people in the shop, and I noticed suddenly that among them, over in the corner, looking at picture postcards of the area, were two young men in uniform. And not the familiar thick khaki of our soldiers' uniforms, or even the slate blue of the RAF. These wore a lighter shade of olive green, and had a sleeker look about them. One was tall and skinny and fair-haired, the other slightly shorter and thick-set. Both had close cropped haircuts under caps of the same olive-green colour. I realised with a little shock that these must be some of the American GIs that Sylvia had been so excited about. The tall fair one was looking across at us, and then came over to the counter. 'Say, excuse me for butting in, but did I hear you say there's no chocolate to be had? Lucky we're here, then. I'm Brad and this is my buddy, Mike. We're both from the Golden State. We have chocolate, plenty of it. Please take some.'

He dived into his pockets and pulled out several chocolate bars. They had shiny brown wrappers and the words Hershey's Milk Chocolate. He turned to me and said, 'How many kids in your family, honey?'

I looked at Auntie Janet, who seemed as taken aback as I was, gulped, and said, 'Well – er – four.'

Brad handed me four bars. Auntie Janet pulled herself together. 'I'm afraid we can't accept them, thank you all the same. Give them back, June.'

I looked from one to the other and at the chocolate bars, inviting in their brown wrapping, but Brad waved them away when I held them out. 'Please take them for your kids, ma'am, courtesy of the US military. Plenty more where they came from. Well, see you around, guys. Cheerio.'

And they were gone, with a tinkle of the bell. May and Auntie Janet and the other customers looked at each other. Someone said ruefully, 'Well, it looks as though the Yanks are here.'

Someone else shook their head. 'And I daresay there'll be trouble, one way or another.'

Chapter Sixteen

Our village did not exactly welcome the American soldiers, not to begin with, anyway. I had noticed already that the local people were always suspicious of anyone new and strange to the area. At first I thought it was because of the war, remembering the slogans that we'd all seen on posters: 'Walls Have Ears' and 'Loose Lips Might Sink Ships' and 'Careless Talk Costs Lives'. But Auntie Janet said it went further back than that. Border people are always wary of strangers, she said, ever since the days the countries of the British Isles were at war with one another. You never knew who might be a spy creeping over the border to gather information and take it back to the enemy on the other side. Which I thought was another proof of how stupid people are to go to war with other people.

Most of the local folk were disapproving, especially when the young GIs began to be seen about the village, looking at the historical buildings like the grey stone church and the remains of the Norman castle, and going to the shop or the little café beside it, where they never drank tea but asked for 'corfee'.

'There's one every way you turn,' grumbled May at the shop. 'And I don't know why they bother coming in here, I really don't. They always seem to have plenty of everything.' But her grumbles were half-hearted, because the Americans were not slow in spending money on anything she had. It had become known that the GIs had things that had been strictly rationed in Britain for a long time, sweets, the delicious Hershey bars, chewing gum. And that they very freely gave them away to children. They laughed good-humouredly when children began hanging around them, hoping for chocolate and chewing gum.

Mr Powell made no secret of his dislike of the Americans, the 'Bloomin' Yanks' as he called them. 'Coming over here, thinking they'll win the war for us and crow about it! Loud and flashy and think they own the place, that's what they're like. Can't stand 'em!'

Auntie Janet had her worries too, though she did not voice them to her husband for fear of increasing his wrath. May had confided in her that the soldiers had brought a supply of women's stockings, feather-light nylon no less. 'So much lighter than silk stockings,' marvelled May, who apparently had been approached by one of the Americans and asked if she'd keep them in her shop and give them out free to the ladies. 'So sheer that you can see right through them! One of 'em had the cheek to pull a pair out of the packet and put his hand inside to show how sheer they was! Indecent, I call it! I told them to be off with their fancy stuff.'

I couldn't help wondering if it would have been different if they had let May sell them in the shop and make a profit. I knew that stockings like these would be a huge attraction for most women. Stockings, especially nylons, were hard to get. I knew that Sylvia would be interested.

It wasn't much use trying to keep things like that a secret, however much Auntie Janet might try. The next school day Sylvia came home buzzing with excitement, she and Helen having encountered a group of GIs as they got off the school bus in the village and exchanged some banter with them. They hadn't accepted anything from them, she was quick to add, seeing her mother's warning look, but I had an idea that it wouldn't have taken much to persuade them. And one of them was so nice, she said, tall and blond and very polite.

'Was he called Brad?' I asked.

She looked annoyed. 'Yes, how did you know? Oh, I see, he was the one who gave you the chocolate. Trust you to go putting yourself forward!'

That was very unfair, I hadn't done that. Auntie Janet quickly intervened. 'It wasn't like that. And I have to say I'm not too keen on you hanging about with those boys, Sylvia. I don't know what your father would say.'

Sylvia tossed her head. 'Oh, *Mother*! Don't be so old-fashioned. We're not in the dark ages! They're our *friends*, for goodness' sake, helping us win the war. Everything has changed since you were young!'

'And not for the better,' said her mother. 'It's wartime, remember? And those Americans are not like us.'

'A good thing too!' said Sylvia. She went off to her bedroom, apparently to do homework, though I knew she was more likely to be looking in the mirror and trying her hair in different styles.

Annie squeezed my arm. 'Don't worry about her! She doesn't think about anything but being an actress and going to Hollywood.'

I wasn't upset about Sylvia. She could have a cutting edge to her tongue but I knew she liked me well enough.

Some of the Americans were in church on Easter Sunday, Brad among them. He remembered us and came over to shake hands with us all and wish us a happy Easter. Mr Powell did not often attend church but he was there that day, being Easter, and he was not best pleased. He shook hands grudgingly when Auntie Janet introduced him, but there were muttered remarks on the way home. 'Bloomin' Yanks! Too darn familiar by half!'

But he had other more important things to worry about than visiting Americans. It was potato planting time and hard work for everyone, even more now that the Boggy Field was drained and ploughed and ready to be planted. Mr Powell bitterly resented the War Ag and the fact that he had been required to grow acre after acre of potatoes, whether he wanted to or not.

'Dad hates the War Ag,' Annie confided to me one night as we got ready for bed. I had gathered that, although I still wasn't quite sure what exactly they did.

'They're supposed to make sure we grow enough food to feed the country, now the ships can't come from abroad,' said Annie. 'Anyway, Dad can't stand them. He says he's got a good mind to get his twelve-bore next time any of their inspectors come snooping round.'

I was mystified. 'What's a twelve-bore?'

'His shotgun. He uses it to shoot rabbits and crows.'

I shivered. Any talk of guns, shooting, bombs or explosions made me feel sick. 'He wouldn't really?'

Annie shrugged. 'No, I don't s'pose so. But he does get hopping mad with them.'

The Boggy Field had been painstakingly ploughed by Mr Powell on his Fordson tractor with the huge metal wheels, and the three-furrow plough behind. I'd watched as he drove up and down the big field, a flock of white gulls wheeling and screaming around his head, ready to dive for any grubs and insects that came to light in the freshly turned earth. He had harrowed the ground to break down the clods, and then ridged it up into raised rows reaching from one hedge to another. Now it had to be planted, each potato dropped into a furrow one foot apart, and that was where we came in, now that the Easter holidays were here. It all had to be done by hand. All of us, even Auntie Janet, toiled up and down the rows, dragging sacks of seed potatoes, dropping them in one at a time and covering them lightly, until our legs ached and our backs felt as though they were breaking. I'd never felt so tired in my life as I did after a day of potato planting. And still there were the animals to be looked after, the household chores to be done.

It was a relief to go back to school, but still only half the field had been planted. Rain had held things up for a day or two, making the ground too soft and sticky to work on. Mr Powell decided that the work was going far too slowly, and that he would have to have more help. No men available, of course. This time, it would have to be Land Girls.

Chapter Seventeen

The Land Girls arrived a few days later, on loan from a farm along the valley where they had been billeted – Daisy and Milly, both glamorous young women despite their uniforms of brown dungarees, tightly belted at the waist, over thick green jumpers. Milly was blonde, although I had a feeling it was what Mum would call bottle-blonde and not her natural colour, as darker roots could be seen at the parting. Daisy was a little younger than Milly, and had a tumbling mass of auburn curls which she tied back with a green-patterned scarf. Milly was from Liverpool and Daisy from Birmingham; both had accents that we found strange and hard to understand. Both wore lipstick, even to work, and both smoked.

'Calms the nerves, chuck,' Milly explained, as we children were inclined to stare as they leaned back in their seats and lit up after dinner on their first day. She put her unlit cigarette in her mouth and leaned forward for Daisy to light it from hers. 'Got an ashtray, love?' she asked Auntie Janet. 'Don't want to drop fag ash all over your nice clean tablecloth.'

Ashtrays were not part of the equipment at the farm, nobody being a smoker, but Auntie Janet produced a saucer for them to tap out the ash. I noticed Sylvia look curiously at the lighted cigarette, and Milly held out the packet to her. 'Want to try one, chuck?'

I saw Auntie Janet purse her lips in disapproval and Sylvia shook her head. I had the feeling her mother thought the Land Girls might be a bad influence on Sylvia. But everyone soon had to admit they were good workers. The potatoes were going in at a rate that pleased even Mr Powell.

He was not so pleased, however, when the news came that there was to be a party in the village hall to celebrate May Day, and that we were all invited.

'It's to welcome the Americans, that's what they're saying,' said Auntie Janet. 'I don't know what to think. From what I've seen, they seem to have no trouble introducing themselves.'

The potato planting would be finished by then, but Milly and Daisy planned to come over for the party.

'It'll be fun, liven the place up a bit,' said Milly. 'I used to love going dancing before the war.' She turned to Sylvia. 'If you like, I could come over and do your hair and make-up for you.'

'Well, we'll need to find out more first,' said Auntie Janet quickly, with a glance at her husband and a warning lift of her eyebrows, meant to convey that he would not approve. It was lost on the girls.

'What's there to find out?' said Milly. 'We just get ourselves dolled up and turn up on the night. Bet those Yanks are boss dancers.'

Mr Powell had been studying the *Farmer and Stockbreeder* and apparently not listening to the chatter, but suddenly became aware of the conversation. His eyebrows came together in a frown, but he only got to his feet, pushed back his chair and said shortly, 'Time to get back to work. Can't sit about all day.'

The two girls looked at each other, grinned and pulled a face, but they stubbed out the last of their cigarettes and followed him out, thanking Auntie Janet for the meal. She looked anxious as she began to clear the table. 'Well, I don't know that getting Land Girls was a good idea. A bit flighty, if you ask me, with their townie ideas, and goodness' knows what kind of families they come from. And this smoke…' She fanned with a dishcloth at the remaining slight haze, looked disapprovingly at the lipstick-smudged cigarette ends, and then returned to her usual brisk self. 'Come on, all of you, just because they're here doesn't mean you don't have to do your bit too. It's Saturday – off you go with them.'

I noticed that all afternoon Sylvia made a point of staying near the two girls and chatting to them across the rows. Her father was too busy with the tractor and the implement that covered the ridges to notice much, but bits of their conversation came across to the rest of us. Sylvia sounded envious when they said they went to the pictures every chance they got. 'Daisy's got a young man, so they go to the flicks together when he's home on leave,' said Milly. 'Me, I'm still footloose and fancy-free. I'm on the lookout, though. Maybe there'll be some talent at this dance. But, hey, we could go out together before that, if you like, the three of us. There's a cinema in town – wonder what they're showing? What do you say, kidda?'

I could see that Sylvia would like nothing more. Whether her parents would give her permission was another thing, though. I had heard them arguing about Sylvia in their bedroom one night some time ago when I'd got up to get a drink of water. I'd lingered for a while, curious to know what it was about. They didn't often disagree. I hoped it was nothing to do with me.

I needn't have worried. It was Sylvia they were discussing. 'She's almost sixteen,' Auntie Janet was saying. 'We can't keep her cooped up here forever, you know. She needs to see some young people, have some fun, even if there is a war on.'

Mr Powell was at his grumpiest after a hard day's work. He said, 'Her head's stuffed full of nonsense, film stars and such. And she's too fond of dolling up, parading herself about…'

Auntie Janet said quietly, 'She doesn't get the chance to do much parading about, wouldn't you say? And she's a pretty girl, she likes to look nice, it's only natural. I don't begrudge her a bit of fun.'

I'd never heard Auntie Janet stand up to her husband so firmly before. It seemed to take the wind out of his sails. He said, sounding less grumpy but very tired, 'Too pretty by half, that's the trouble. Only trying to keep her out of the way of trouble…'

'I know.' Auntie Janet's voice had softened. 'You want to keep us all safe. It's this war, gets all our nerves on edge. Go to sleep now.'

I stole away, beginning to feel guilty for eavesdropping.

To our astonishment, Sylvia was allowed to go to the cinema with Daisy and Milly. She came back glowing.

'It was *The Grapes of Wrath.'* She came into our room and sat on the end of Annie's bed to describe it in detail. 'Oh my, I've never seen anything so tragic! The injustice of it! This poor farming family were turned out of their farm and had to trail across America to try to find work. And Henry Fonda – wow, what can I say! And guess what? Mum and Dad will let me go to the dance with Daisy and Milly! Wonders will never cease!'

She was slightly less pleased when we heard that we three younger ones had been invited as well, even Tom, who had had a sudden spurt of growth and could now look down on both Annie and me, to his great glee. Their parents seemed happier that we'd all be going together.

'To keep an eye on each other,' said Annie.

I had never been to a grown-up party and had no idea what to expect. The first consideration for all of us was what we would wear.

The potatoes were all planted now and were waiting for a visit from the War Ag inspector. The Land Girls were no longer needed, but they had promised they would come over when they had a spare evening, and, true to their word, they turned up on bicycles on a breezy evening that tossed the newly budded apple blossom and scattered its petals like white snowflakes. They had discarded their Land Army uniforms and wore slacks and light jumpers.

The contents of our wardrobes did not impress them. 'Yikes, nothing much there to suit,' said Daisy, rejecting the meagre collection of overalls, jumpers, pleated skirts and sensible shoes that comprised Annie's and my wardrobe. Even our Sunday-best dresses merited no more than a sniff. I'd already outgrown mine anyway. Neither was Milly any more impressed with Sylvia's apparel.

'I've been making myself a dress,' volunteered Sylvia, bringing out the home-made, rose-sprigged frock.

'Hmm, nice one, kidda. That might do for June maybe, if we let it out a bit at the waist. You need something a bit more glam. I know, there's a couple of weeks yet. We'll put all our coupons together and see what we can do. I'm sure between us we can run something up. Dab hand with a needle, is our Daisy.'

The girls might be a touch flighty but you couldn't fault them for being kind and generous, as Auntie Janet had to admit. They cycled into town, bought material, cut and sewed and pinned and fitted, spending hours of their precious free time kitting us out, as Milly said, making us fit to be seen. In the end, each of us had an outfit that transformed us from farm girls in overalls to young ladies in dresses, who'd make those Yanks sit up and take notice, said Milly – though not in the hearing of Auntie Janet and her husband.

Chapter Eighteen

I felt shivers of anticipation as we got ready for the big event. For a few days I'd had the feeling that I didn't really want to go, that I'd much rather stay home and go for a walk in the newly green countryside. But the enthusiasm of the two Land Girls and Sylvia was infectious.

We took turns to inspect ourselves in the only full-length mirror in the house, on the door of the wardrobe in Mr and Mrs Powell's bedroom. Annie's dress was moss green, which suited her red-gold hair and green eyes; it had short sleeves and Milly had made a matching hairband from a scrap of spare material. Mine was the rose-patterned one, artfully altered to fit by Daisy's nimble fingers. The sweetheart neckline and puffed sleeves made me look older, and Milly had found a narrow pink belt for the waist, which gave me a shape that no longer looked like a little girl's. Sylvia's dress took our breath away – forget-me-not blue, the exact colour of her eyes, fitted bodice, padded shoulders and a little frill below the waist that we were told was called a peplum. She looked like a film star already, especially when the girls had applied a little discreet make-up and done her hair in finger-waves. Sylvia had hung about May's shop a couple of times the week before; I had a hunch that she was hoping to acquire a pair of the coveted nylon stockings if there happened to be any being given away. She was asking for trouble there, I thought – if her dad had found out he'd have locked her up before he let her go to the party. So no nylons had come her way.

'And I don't even have a pair of decent silk stockings!' she wailed.

'Soon fixed,' said Milly. She went to the bag she had brought and pulled out a little pot of something and a small brush. 'Skin paint,' she said. 'Just a nice discreet touch. And could you ask your mum for a bit of gravy browning, Annie?'

I'd never seen anyone paint their legs before, but Sylvia was stood upon a chair, told to hitch up her skirt, and her long slender legs were given a coat of a pale tan paint. To finish it off, Milly carefully painted a stripe of gravy browning up the backs of the legs where the seams would be.

'There!' she said triumphantly. 'How about that! Just make sure nobody spills anything over you or it'll smudge. And hope it doesn't rain. Anyone else for a leg job?'

Annie and I declined. Painted legs might be a step too far for us. Our white ankle socks would have to do.

Auntie Janet had a look that was almost wistful as she surveyed us in all our finery. 'Doesn't seem so long ago that I was getting ready to go dancing,' she said. Looking at her weather-beaten features, the roughness of her hard-working hands, the old flowered pinafore, I could hardly believe she ever had. Compared with my mum, who still had permanent waves and wore lipstick, she seemed so old and careworn. Buoyed up with the excitement of the evening, I went over and gave her a hug, something I had never done before. 'Thank you for everything you do for me.' She seemed surprised and flustered, but I could see she was pleased too. She said, 'You're very welcome, I'm sure. You're a good girl, June.'

Auntie Janet drove us to the village hall in the old truck, which had been specially cleaned for the occasion, Sylvia in front, so her dress would not get crushed, she said, the three of us squeezed into the back with Tom in the middle and our dresses taking their chances. There were blackout curtains at the windows, but inside was another world, a world of light, colour and music from a three-piece band that had been drafted in from town. The room was already full, the uniforms of the GIs mingling with girls in pretty summer dresses and excited children running around getting in everyone's way. There was food at one end, on a long table presided over by a group of mature ladies, who were keeping a watchful eye on the proceedings. Daisy and Milly had come on ahead after attending to our toilettes and their own, and were already chatting to some of the soldiers over glasses of lemonade. We had been assured that there were to be no stronger drinks on offer. As soon as the band struck up a lively dance tune, the Land Girls were the first on the floor, dancing with each other. It wasn't long before a couple of the Americans came over and asked if they could partner them instead. Then another approached Sylvia and asked her to dance. She smiled charmingly and allowed herself to join the couples now taking to the floor. Annie, Tom and I stood awkwardly near the refreshments table, sipping our lemonade and nibbling cheese straws. Then one of Annie's friends whirled over and grabbed her by the hand. 'Come on, don't be shy!' That left Tom and myself. He looked at me.

'Er – do you want to dance?'

'You mean with you?' I asked, very ungraciously.

'Well, course, who else is there?' he said truculently.

I felt sorry for him, being stuck with me and having to be polite. Tom looked older since he'd grown and was considerably taller than me now. He was wearing new long trousers and a white shirt, his dark hair brushed neatly, and I noticed again what beautiful eyes he had, green like Annie's, flecked with brown and with long dark lashes. He was at that awkward stage I'd noticed with boys, when their voices had deepened but sometimes still squeaked embarrassingly, but he was becoming quite a nice-looking boy.

'OK, then, let's dance,' I said.

Neither of us was particularly good at it, but we did our best and I felt we had not made too much of a spectacle of ourselves. The music had changed from popular dance tunes like 'In the Mood' and 'Moonlight Becomes You' and taken on a different kind of beat that brought a new excitement. Some of the Americans were teaching their partners new steps, jerky and quick instead of slow and sentimental, pulling them close and then pushing them away, and every now and then twirling them around in a circle.

'It's called jitterbugging,' said Milly, who had stopped by to get a drink. She was pink-cheeked and bright-eyed. 'It's real good fun. You should try it. I'm going to.'

It did look exciting, but a bit daunting too. I was sure I'd fall over and make a fool of myself if anyone tried to twirl me round. I was watching the couples when a sudden disturbance broke out at the other side of the room. Two of the olive-green-clad Americans appeared to be fighting. Others were gathering round and I could see Sylvia's blue dress and blonde head among them. I saw that one of the fighting men was a crew-cut redhead and that the other was dark-skinned with kinky black hair. I'd noticed that there were two or three black soldiers among the others, mostly keeping to themselves in a tight little group. Most of us hadn't seen many black people before and they were getting stared at a lot. I tried hard to remember my manners and not keep looking. But I found myself being pushed forward by others crowding to see. Sylvia seemed to be in the forefront, looking flushed and alarmed.

'What's happening?' said someone at my elbow.

'He asked that blonde girl to dance,' said a girl I didn't know. 'Sylvia Powell, I think her name is. Seems it's not allowed.'

Why on earth not? I wondered. Then I saw a familiar face – Brad. I hadn't noticed him before, all the Americans looking much the same in their olive-green uniforms. He saw me at the same moment. 'June! You OK?'

I nodded. 'Yes. What are they fighting about?'

'Well – it's a bit awkward, see. Things are different over here and some of the boys don't like it.'

'How do you mean?'

He looked across to where the two fighting soldiers had been pulled apart. The dark-skinned one returned to his group, looking sullen, while the other joined his mates, both of them straightening their ties and adjusting their uniforms, looking, I thought, like a pair of ruffled fighting cockerels smoothing their feathers.

'You see, back home, blacks and whites don't mix,' said Brad, a little awkwardly. 'Seems that black guy asked your sister to dance, and Chip there took exception.'

I felt I should have corrected him and said that Sylvia was not my sister, but I was trying to get my head round the rest of it.

'But you're all in the army together,' I said.

'Yeah, I know. But it's different back home – I'm not saying it's right, but that's how it is.' He looked down at his feet.

Sylvia came over, pink and flustered. 'Those two were actually fighting – over me! I was never so embarrassed!'

She didn't look embarrassed to me – rather, excited, I thought. I wondered what her father would have to say about the incident. She must have had the same thought, for she clapped her hands to her mouth and paled a little. 'Don't breathe a word to Dad, will you?'

Before I could reply, she had spotted Brad next to me. 'Oh, hi there.'

Brad gave a little bow. Whatever their differences, these boys had perfect manners. 'Good evening, Miss Sylvia. Now the excitement's over, would you care to dance?'

And they were away, forgetting me completely, which left me a little disgruntled. I'd like to have known more about why black people and white ones were treated differently in America.

The evening wasn't exactly spoiled by the incident, but the atmosphere took on a different tone somehow, for me at least. Tom and I dutifully danced together a couple of times more, and Annie and I even tried jitterbugging. I wished Brad had asked me to dance, but he didn't. I must seem just a kid to him, I thought, and told myself it didn't matter anyway.

And later that night, when Auntie Janet had picked us up at the appointed time, and I was tucked up in bed listening to Annie's gentle snoring, I pondered again on the strangeness of things. Americans were our allies, we could be friends with them. But not too good friends, apparently. And if their skins were black, not at all, it seemed. White skin good, black skin bad, I thought. Blue eyes good, dark eyes bad. But Conrad had blue eyes and blond hair, and so had Brad. And they were bitter enemies. Why can't we all just get along? I thought. My mind was getting muddled and my thoughts were still in a whirl as I drifted off to sleep.

Interlude
Juniper

'It isn't fair, is it,' I said to Dad that evening, 'that people are treated differently because of their skin colour, or where they live, or how rich or how poor they are. I mean, there's enough of everything in the world for everyone to have what they need, isn't there? Why can't people get along, and share?'

Dad was watching a news programme on TV. He sighed. 'Honey, this old world is an unfair place. Some things can't be helped, but a lot of things are down to greed and pride. We like to have money and power and possessions. We like to be successful. We like to hold on to what we have. We like to think our country is better than others. I guess we have to be thankful that we're the lucky ones.'

'Well, I don't want to be like that,' I said. 'I'm not going to be greedy. I'm going to do something, something that will help to make everything more fair.'

I really hadn't a clue what I was talking about, but listening to Nana's story had made me suddenly aware of the injustice of so many things, and a little ashamed of my own privileged lifestyle.

Dad laughed. 'You're becoming quite the little crusader! You sound just like your Nana! Has she told you about the *things she did, the missionaries she supports, the organisation she set up, she and her husband, to bring together people from warring nations? Reconcile, it was called.'*

I'd never heard of it, and Nana hadn't told me any of that. But, getting deeper into her story every day, it didn't surprise me. It really didn't surprise me at all.

Chapter Nineteen

June

As May came in, the countryside was so beautiful that it took my breath away. Green exploded upon green, every shade imaginable from the deeper green of oak leaves to the light yellowy lichens on the old walls of the farmhouse, and every possible shade in between. Buds on trees burst into tender green leaves, grass sprang up from the verges and ditches, jostling for space with young nettles and dock leaves, which Auntie Janet said always grew close to each other because dock leaf juice was a soothing remedy for nettle stings. The bare brown hedges sprouted out fresh green growth, every bush, plant, weed, stem, springing up anew, green piled upon green. Feathery ferns uncurled along the stream bank, adding their graceful fronds to the wonderful textures and shades of the same colour.

The apple trees and the cherry and plums in the orchard had pink and white blossom that drifted and floated when there was wind, and the hawthorn by the yard gate was covered with a froth of sweet-smelling, creamy-white blossom in which bumble bees buzzed sleepily, half-drunk with the fragrance and the nectar.

Soon the hedgerows and ditches were starred with the graceful cow parsley, tall red campion, delicate blue vetches, lacy white stitchwort. I borrowed a book from the school library and learned all the names. And the little spinney at the bottom of the Boggy Field was suddenly carpeted with bluebells under a canopy of fresh green beech leaves. Swallows had flown back from foreign parts and were nesting under the eaves of the big barn. Not even the ugliness of war could stop the spring returning and bringing life and beauty back to the countryside.

I couldn't get enough of it. Looking back over the past months, I was amazed at how I'd been, the way I'd hated the loneliness, the hard work, the mud. Now I thought this must be the most beautiful place on earth. I'd got into the habit of walking into the fields and around the hedgerows every evening after tea, now that the days were longer and the evenings lighter. There was a special place I loved to sit for a while, at the edge of the bluebell spinney where a little stream ran through. Sylvia, Tom and Annie thought I was a bit odd; they couldn't see any point in walking around just looking at things they'd seen every day of their lives and mostly taken for granted. But every newly uncurling fern frond, every new wildflower I noticed, every glimpse of a bird's nest in some thick bush, was a source of wonder to me. I made a point of taking the wildflower book with me, to be able to put a name to each new flower I saw, some with such interesting names – germander speedwell, scarlet pimpernel, ragged robin, herb robert, yellow rattle. But most of all, I loved the green.

I paused by the gate of the Boggy Field one evening after my stroll and stood leaning on the gate and looking back over the field. It was boggy no longer. Thanks largely to the efforts of prisoners of war and Land Girls, it now held ridged rows of newly sprouted potato plants, just showing their dark green leaves through the soil. The leaves were poisonous, I had been told, and so were the potatoes if they were allowed to stay in the light and turn green. I pondered on the strangeness of things – thinking of delicious mashed potatoes, crispy roast potatoes, potatoes cooked in their jackets – how the same plant could produce both nourishing food and deadly poison, depending on how you used it. I also remembered the back-breaking task of planting the potatoes one by one.

I hadn't heard anyone approach until there was the sound of someone clearing their throat. I jumped. It was Mr Powell, or Uncle Bill, as I was supposed to call him but couldn't quite bring myself to do.

'Nice evenin',' he said, by way of greeting, which I'd noticed was the usual way country people began a conversation, adapted if it was a different time of day, or if it was raining or foggy or blowing a gale.

I agreed. Long shadows were stretching across the field, and there was a hint of red sky, which heralded a fine day tomorrow. He came and leaned on the gate beside me, looking across the field. 'Taters are up.'

I agreed again, wishing I could think of something else to say. He went on, gloomily, 'Weeds comin' up too. A lot of hoeing, that means. May have to get those Land Girls back.' He sighed heavily, which gave me the impression that to him the Land Girls had been a mixed blessing.

To cheer him up, I said impulsively, 'I'll help with the hoeing,' although I had no real idea of what kind of work it was.

He turned and looked at me, and I saw how lined his face was under the tan, with deep furrows across his forehead and round his eyes and mouth. His eyes were like Tom's and Annie's, green flecked with brown, and he might have been a handsome man once, before work and worry wore him down. He sighed again, and said, 'You're a game gel, I'll say that. Do you miss London and the bright lights?'

I thought for a moment, and said truthfully, 'Not much. There's no bright lights anyway, it's all blacked out. I hated the bombs. But I do miss my mum and dad.' I added quickly, 'But I like it here.' And then, in a burst of confidence, I added, 'I really love it.'

He smiled, and all the grumpiness and weariness seemed gone, just for a moment. Then the sadness came back. 'I love it too. Oh, it was great, when me and the missus started out. Hard work, but we weren't afraid of that. We built up a fine dairy herd of Friesians, one of the best for miles around.' He waved his hand towards the next field, also planted with potatoes. 'All that and most of my other land as well were fine cow pastures. We'd keep up some grass for hay every year, and graze the rest. Good, rich grass – ryegrass, foxtail, timothy grass, and a good sprinkling of fescue. May and June it'd be a sight to see, full of meadowsweet, vetches and red and white clover. I never had to use much of that chemical fertiliser, just some basic slag in the spring and good old cow muck when we ploughed up a field and reseeded. It'd be a joy to see. And when the cows and calves were turned out after the winter, well, what capers they got up to, gallopin' and jumpin' all over the field, even the old 'uns.' He paused. I'd never heard such a long speech from him before. His face, which had become bright and animated, saddened again. 'All gone now. Cows, and their pastures.'

I felt I should offer some kind of sympathy, and said, 'Was it the War Ag?' I still didn't quite understand about the War Ag, but I'd heard it mentioned so many times and often blamed for most things that went wrong.

His face darkened. 'Aye. Bunch of crooks, that's my opinion. There's supposed to be farmers among 'em, but if that's true I reckon they're mostly gentleman farmers with a big acreage and not much common sense or idea of proper farming. The sort that never gets their hands dirty. I'd just got my place up and running, bit of profit coming in at long last, beautiful pastureland, beautiful herd. And what do they do? Take my cows, except them two old milkers. Say plough up your fields and plant potatoes. Acres of potatoes, to feed the country, they say. And my flock of sheep as well, every one. Even took my good old sheepdog.'

I'd heard of people having to give up their pets, dogs and cats, because they ate food that might be needed by humans. I remembered Mrs Wilkins next door back home, crying one day because her spaniel had to be put to sleep. Rabbits were allowed to be kept, but only if they were fed on leftover vegetable waste and eventually used for food themselves. I could see that Mr Powell really mourned the loss of his livestock, and of his beautiful grassy meadows.

'Officious beggars, coming with their records and their clipboards and their puffed-up important ideas of theirselves. Little Hitlers, I call 'em,' he said bitterly.

'What would have happened if you'd refused to do it?' I asked.

He turned and squinted against the rays of the setting sun. 'We'd be turned out – out of our own farm, mind you! We wouldn't stand a chance. One feller did refuse. It was in all the papers. Man in his sixties, farmed his place for years, he had, refused to leave. Got his shotgun and threatened them when they come to evict him.'

'What happened?'

'They shot him dead. Or anyhow, shot him, and he died of his injuries.'

I felt a shiver go down my spine. I remembered Annie telling me that her father sometimes threatened to take his shotgun to the War Ag men. I hoped, how I hoped, that he never would, however badly he felt.

But I felt a sudden warmth towards Mr Powell that I never had before. I said, 'It's the war, isn't it? I hate the war!'

He turned and looked at me and his face softened. 'I forget your dad is away fighting. Sorry for going on, like. It's just, evenin's like these, you tend to remember how things was.'

The sun was sinking in a red ball below the skyline. Birds were twittering sleepily in the hedgerow by the gate.

'It's still beautiful, though,' I said, and hoped it would be some comfort to him.

Chapter Twenty

It did not take long for Mr Powell to be back in a grumpy mood again. Two things happened on the same day that threw him into a bad mood. The first was the official letter from the War Ag giving notice that they would be coming to inspect the growing crops of potatoes the following week. The second was that everyone in the village, including us, had been asked to a party at the American base, a chance for them to repay the hospitality that they had been shown.

'Bloomin' jumped-up Yanks, flaunting theirselves and their goods, thinkin' they're so superior to the likes of us,' was his opinion, voiced for the benefit of anyone who would listen. 'I thought as they'd come over to help us win the war. Not doing much about it, as I can see. Not doin' much at all, except dancin' and fightin' atween theirselves. Too well fed, that's their trouble, and not enough work.'

Somehow, the word had reached his ears that there had been a fight at the welcoming gathering in the village hall, although mercifully he seemed to have no idea that Sylvia had been involved.

'They're training, Dad,' said Tom. 'We see them out doing exercises most days when we're coming home on the bus from school.'

'Exercises, pah! They can come and get some exercise hoeing those spuds before the inspector comes, if they wants something to do.'

There was no reasoning with him. The weeds were growing as thick and fast as everything else, and already the hopeful potato plants were in danger of getting smothered by a growth of grass and chickweed and another weed called fat hen. It had rained for a few days and been impossible to hoe. But now it was drying, and it was possible to get on the ground again without trampling down the soil and bringing great clods home on our boots. The Land Girls had been promised for the following week; until then we must make a start ourselves. The growth between the rows had been scuffled out mechanically, our job was to weed out the unwanted growth between the plants on the ridges. I soon found that hoeing was hard work, although it did not involve so much bending and stooping. What it did involve, as I soon found, was blisters on the hands. And we were in a warm spell. I was mightily relieved, when, after what seemed like an age of toil, with all of us, Land Girls and family alike, working hour after hour, the job was finally done.

Every evening now I escaped by myself into the green world of the hedgerows and fields and woodland, the space and the freedom and the peace, to my special place at the edge of the small spinney where the bluebells were, where the stream trickled through a ditch lined with ferns and tall grass. The weather had stayed dry for the last week or so, so the stream bed had dried, but in the shade the undergrowth remained green and lush. I had thought that in the summer I would dabble my feet in the stream and enjoy the coolness but I could see that it was likely that the stream bed would be dry all summer, unless there was torrential rain to make it flow again. Even so, it was very pleasant to kick off my Wellington boots and socks and wiggle my toes in the long cool grass. Wellies were necessary for any job on the farm, but they did not allow feet to breathe. I stretched out my toes, leaned back and breathed a sigh of relief. A small spotted ladybird crawled off a nearby dock leaf and onto my hand. I looked at its little body, such a shiny red that it seemed to have been painted on, and decorated with seven black spots. Mr Powell, or Uncle Bill, as I now called him since our evening chat, had told me ladybirds were good, they fed on the aphids which ate crops and could make the difference between a good crop and a very poor one. I did not move a muscle, and in a moment, the ladybird opened a pair of tiny painted wings and disappeared in the vegetation.

I lay on my back and almost dozed. Above me, beech and hazel boughs creaked gently in a slight breeze and their leaves made shifting patterns in the sunlight. I closed my eyes, letting the aches of the day ease and fade. The leaves whispered gently.

And then suddenly I came fully awake. Another sound had come, not the twittering of birds in the bushes or the rustle of moving leaves. A human sound.

I sat up, listening. All the family were back in the farmhouse, I knew. Nobody else should be here. Uncle Bill said that poachers sometimes came around, after rabbits or pheasants or partridges. But this wasn't a voice, exactly. More like a sigh, or a groan.

I listened. There it was again, faint, but unmistakably a groan, and not far away. In fact, the sound seemed to come from somewhere very close to the ground, or even under it.

I thought of the horror stories Tom sometimes read and related to Annie and me, of people buried alive, or strange creatures who lived in underground caves. My heart began to race.

I quickly yanked on my boots and got up, very cautiously, undecided for a moment. Part of me wanted to run back to the farmhouse, to tell someone what I'd heard, let them decide what to do. But something made me hesitate. There was pain in that sound. Something, or someone, was nearby, and they were in pain.

I followed the dry stream bed in the direction of the sound. A little way along, a kind of outcrop of rock reached part way over, bordered by tall ferns and long grass that covered the stream bed for a few yards. I was sure that the sound had come from there. I crept closer, heart racing, bent over and parted the long grass. Beneath the jutting stone there was a sudden movement and a very human intake of breath. I pulled back more vegetation, and suddenly found myself staring into a pair of blue eyes in a face white and drawn with pain. I could see only part of the person, a vague shape lying stretched out and hidden in the ditch under the greenery, but I recognised that person at once.

There was another gasp, and a weak voice said, 'Choon!'

Suddenly the fear left me. 'Conrad! Why are you here? What's happened?'

He asked weakly, 'Are you alone?' and when I nodded, he gave a long sigh of relief. '*Danke Gott*! Choon, I need help. I have escaped from the camp. They will be searching and I must run but I have hurt my ankle and I cannot…'

My head was whirling as I tried to take this in. 'But – but – why did you escape? How? Why did you come here?'

'That can wait. Choon, for now I need help. I should have been far away by now if I could have travelled all night as I intended, but I twisted my ankle and I cannot walk on it. I was taking a shortcut across your farm to get to the station in the village. From there I hoped to hide on the early train, then get another and maybe to the coast by nightfall. But now…' He dragged himself part way out of the ditch and gave a moan of pain.

'Let me look at it.' I scrambled down further into the ditch and he pulled himself up on his elbows and heaved himself out from under the sheltering rock. His ankle above the dirty sock was swollen and a horrible purplish-red colour. It seemed to be twisted at an odd angle. He grimaced. 'I took off my boot, fool that I am, and now I cannot get it back on again.'

I prodded gingerly at the ankle. 'It may be broken. It looks kind of twisted.'

He nodded. 'Yes. I caught it in a rabbit hole, running. There was a crack. I tried to keep going but it was no good. I crawled across the last two fields until I found this ditch to hide in.'

'Have you been here all this time?'

He nodded. 'I thought I'd try again when it was dark. But now…' He pulled a face.

I pulled myself together. Conrad was hurt, he was in danger, and there was no one but me he could turn to for help. I felt sure Uncle Bill would turn him in if he knew. 'What would happen if you were caught?' I asked.

He looked at me and shrugged. 'I do not know. But I do not want to find out.' His face turned very sad.

Whatever it was, he would be punished. He might even be shot. I shivered. I would not let that happen. 'Right,' I said, thankful that I'd attended First Aid classes for a while back in London. 'First thing, we have to bind that ankle and bring down the swelling.' I cast around for something to use as a binder. I had on last week's school blouse under my jumper and dungarees. That would do.

'If you look the other way,' I said. 'I'll take off my blouse.'

He obediently closed his eyes and turned his head. Dressed again, I tore the blouse into rough strips. Goodness knows how I'd explain to Auntie Janet. As gently as I could, I wrapped the makeshift bandage firmly about the ankle, finding a safety pin on my dungarees that was replacing a lost button, to fasten it. He winced with pain but smiled when it was done.

'Ah, *danke*! *Danke schön*! It feels better already!'

What next? I wondered. I could not leave him lying in a ditch. He would need shelter, water, food. I wondered if I could help him to the farm, to one of the buildings, but decided it would not be possible. Someone would be sure to see, or find him there. But there was the hut at the bottom of the Boggy Field, where the POWs had sheltered when they worked here. It wasn't used now. It would do, at least for the time being until I could figure out the next step. Not once did I even consider turning him in.

The hut was not far away, although there was a hedge between. 'If I help you, we could try to get through the hedge to the hut,' I said. 'I'll try to find a thin place and mend it afterwards. You can't stay in the ditch – look, it's still damp.'

He smiled faintly. 'I know. It's soaked through my clothes.'

With a great deal of effort, between us we got him to his feet. He leaned heavily on me as we hobbled along the hedgerow, keeping close to it, and found what looked like a weak spot. Getting him through was still difficult, and involved a lot of crashing and breaking of twigs, leaving the weak place considerably weaker than before. But we were through, and there in the corner of the field was the hut. Dragging the injured ankle and still leaning on me, Conrad staggered across to it. I prayed Uncle Bill was not out looking at his fields, although it was beginning to grow dark and he was usually inside with his boots off by now. Auntie Janet and the others would wonder where I was, though. They might come looking. We'd have to hurry.

The inside of the hut smelled musty. Some loose straw lay scattered about; a cloud of dust rose from it and made us both sneeze when I piled it in a heap. Conrad sank down on it with a sigh of relief. At least the roof was sound in case of rain, I thought.

'Listen,' I said. 'I'll have to go but I'll try to sneak out later, when they're asleep, and bring you some food and water. I'll try to find some aspirin for the pain. Maybe by tomorrow night you'll be able to walk again.'

I did not think it very likely, but I had run out of ideas of what to do.

'*Danke*, Choon,' he said weakly. 'Thank you. Water, please, if nothing else. I'm very thirsty.'

I fumbled in my pockets and found a couple of squashed-looking toffees. They were all I had. I gave them to him, and hoped they would help a little. I slipped out, closing the door carefully, and back through the hedge, patching it up as best I could with twigs and branches. I had almost reached the orchard when I heard voices calling my name.

'June! Ju-une! Oh, there you are!'

Annie and Tom were running towards the orchard gate, waving their arms. I tried to seem as nonchalant as possible and hoped I didn't look too bedraggled. They were so excited they wouldn't have noticed anyway. They skidded to a halt beside me.

'Guess what?' said Annie, and before she could go on, Tom was interrupting.

'One of the prisoners from the POW camp has escaped! We heard it on the news. There's a big search on!'

Interlude

Juniper

Dad pounced on me that evening, as I came out of my room after writing the day's notes.

'Juni! I wanted a word with you. Vacation plans!'

'Huh?' I felt slightly dazed, still half in the dangerous world of Britain in the 1940s.

'Yes, all planned. Starting next week, road trip, just the three of us. Maybe we'll head for Arizona and the Grand Canyon. What do you think?'

'Uh, yeah, cool.'

'You don't sound very excited. We thought you'd love it, some real adventure after what must have been a pretty dull week for you. Nearly over now, though. Maybe we could get Luciana to cover tomorrow with Nana and you could go to a friend for the day, just for a change. Unless you really want to be with Nana again.'

'You bet I do!' I said.

Chapter Twenty-one

June

I went to bed that night with my head in a whirl. The household was abuzz with the news of the escaped prisoner. Sylvia inclined to be a little hysterical about it all.

'It's dreadful! He's from that camp the ones that worked here were from! What if it's one of them? What if he comes here?'

'Now why on earth would he do that?' said her mother sensibly. 'He'll want to put as much distance as he can between him and the camp, I should think. Poor chap, whatever made him do such a thing, I wonder. He hasn't got a chance, they'll have dogs and all sorts out on his trail, I expect.'

Sylvia shuddered dramatically. 'All the same, I'm not going out on my own. You never know!'

'What would happen if he was caught?' asked Annie, and Tom drew an invisible line across his throat.

'Kaput!'

I gave a shiver. Auntie Janet looked at me. 'Be quiet, Tom. You're frightening June, and there's no need. Take no notice, June. But may be as well not to wander off too much on your own, or not until we hear this man's recaptured, anyway.'

'He won't get far, I'll warrant,' said Uncle Bill.

The party at the American base was to be the following evening. Auntie Janet shooed us off to bed early. Uncle Bill was still humphing and muttering about it, but he had agreed to let the four of us go. Annie was wound up with excitement, what with the escaped prisoner and the coming party, and I thought she'd never settle down and go to sleep.

'I'm looking forward to it, aren't you?'

I grunted, and pretended to be half-asleep.

'It's a pity we have to wear the same dresses,' Annie prattled on. 'Do you think Milly and Daisy will come over and help us with our hair again?'

I gave a faint snore that I hoped was realistic. Annie wasn't fooled. 'I know you're not asleep! What's the matter with you, June? You've been kind of odd this evening. Does thinking about that escaped prisoner bother you? I think it's quite exciting, don't you? Livens things up around here a bit. June! Ju-une!'

It was no use pretending. I turned over and said, in what I hoped was a weak voice, 'Annie, I don't want to talk. I have a splitting headache and I want to try to sleep.'

Annie was fooled this time. 'Oh, sorry! Shall I go and get some aspirin for you?'

I was about to say no, then I thought, why not? It would be one less thing to get together for Conrad. I said, 'Uh, yes please. Bring the whole packet. I might have to take another dose in the night.'

'Well, make sure you leave enough time between the doses. Mum says if you overdose on aspirin it makes your stomach bleed.'

But she got out of bed and fetched the whole packet, along with a drink of water. I pretended to gulp down a couple of tablets.

Annie went to sleep at last. We had a little alarm clock with luminous hands in our room. When they pointed to 11.30 and the house had been quiet for some time, I decided to make a move. I climbed out of bed and pulled on dungarees and jumper over my pyjamas. Taking a big step to avoid the stair that creaked, I stole downstairs to the quiet kitchen. It was a dark night, just a new crescent moon showed a sliver of light in the black sky. I found a bag behind the pantry door; it was one of Auntie Janet's shopping bags but I'd make sure I put it back afterwards. I investigated the meat safe and stone slabs in the dairy. Half a ham was there, with some slices already cut, perfect. I wrapped them in the greaseproof paper Auntie Janet used for butter, and managed to break off part of a hunk of cheese. There was bread in the crock, a whole loaf, and – joy! – the heel of another one, which I added to the bag. There were strawberries in a bowl; a handful would surely not be missed. I took a couple of rock cakes from the batch Auntie Janet had baked today. Now, water. He'd said he needed water more than anything. Plenty in the scullery. There were several bottles of home-made elderflower cordial standing on the cold slab, most of them full, but one of them was half-empty. I knew what I'd do. I'd fill the bottle up with water and take it for Conrad. The bottles made a tiny clink as one touched another and I froze for a moment, listening. Nothing stirred. I quickly filled up the bottle from the tap, pulled on my boots, picked up the bag and let myself out of the back door.

I'd never been outside the farmhouse alone at night, except for that one time I'd foolishly decided to run away. I remembered how Uncle Bill and Tom had come to search for me, and how Uncle Bill's strong arms had carried me home. What would they say if they knew what I was doing now? Stealing food and taking it to an enemy. Would they brand me a traitor and a thief? Were there punishments for those who helped the enemy?

But these kinds of thoughts wouldn't help anyone. And I was not going to let Conrad suffer pain and hunger if I could help it. He might be the enemy but he was also my friend.

Everything looked different at night. The thin light of the young moon turned familiar buildings into looming dark shapes, the colours were gone, trees and bushes that I knew and loved were ominous ragged shapes against the sky. Anything might be hiding in the shadows. I slipped silently across the yard, into the cow pasture and then through the gate into the Boggy Field, heading for the distant corner by the wood where the hut was. I'd hurried effortlessly across the grassy meadow, but the ridged soil and rows of potatoes slowed me down and made me stumble and slip. I prayed that Uncle Bill would not notice any damage to his neat rows. Thank goodness the hoeing was done and nobody would be working in the field for a while.

Heart thumping, I pushed open the door of the hut, which creaked and groaned. For a moment there was total darkness and silence, then my eyes became accustomed to the faint light from the grimy window. There was a rustle in the straw and a whispered question: 'Choon?'

'Yes, it's me,' I said. 'I've brought food. How is the ankle, Conrad?'

More shuffling as he pulled himself up to a sitting position, and then a gasp of pain. 'Still not good.'

I sat down beside him and opened the bag. 'I brought aspirin. And drink.'

'Ah, drink!' He seized upon the bottle and drank from it as though his very life depended upon it. Maybe it did, if he hadn't had a drink since he'd escaped. I gave him some aspirin and left the packet with him. 'But don't take too many at once, or it'll make your stomach bleed.'

'*Nein, Mutter.*' I could sense him grinning in the dimness. I pulled out the food, which he began to devour ravenously. 'Thank you, thank you, Choon,' he said with his mouth full.

'I'll bring more tomorrow night,' I said, and then hesitated. 'If I can.'

I'd remembered that tomorrow night was the party at the American base, and that I'd gathered the adults had been invited too. I wondered if I could make some excuse to stay home. Maybe I could say my headache had got worse. But I knew it was hopeless. One of them would insist on staying home with me. Besides, maybe he would be able to move on by then.

'Do you think your ankle is getting better?' I asked.

He sighed. 'I am afraid not. I tried to stand and walk a little, but could not. I could feel the bones grating together. The leg will not bear my weight. I fear I did more damage yesterday keeping going after it was injured. Maybe I should have given myself up then.'

We had to think of a plan. Was there anyone I could trust to smuggle Conrad out and see him on his way? I was afraid not. And then the army would be out searching for him anyway. I heard myself say, 'I think you're better staying here and lying low for a few days. Maybe they'll think you've got clear away by now and give up looking. I'll bring more food and water at night...'

He finished the bread he had been chewing and wrapped up the rest carefully in the greaseproof paper. I could see the shape of him now my eyes were accustomed to the dimness, shoulders slumped, injured leg stretched out in front. He said, 'I'm sorry you got mixed up in this, Choon. I hope you will not get into trouble.'

I hoped so too, but said quickly, 'I won't, don't worry.' And then to change the subject, I said, 'Why did you escape, anyway?'

He sighed again, long and heavily. 'It was not planned. There was a man, one of the guards. He hates us Germans. All day long he mocks us, goads us, especially the young ones. He's a bully. He pushes us to our limits. There's one boy, barely my age, and very homesick. That man constantly harries him until he cries in his sleep at night. I just could not take it any longer. I shouted at that guard and told him what I thought, that he's a pig of a man. He hit me. And I hit him back. I knocked him out, I think, he was groaning on the floor. Others came, there was a scuffle and a lot of confusion. All in a minute, I decided I would run, so I did, while they were still confused, trying to work out what had happened. Others covered my escape and I made it over the fence and out of the camp – they are not as securely guarded as ours are, I have heard – and got into the woodland. I don't know how soon I was missed but I kept going. I had some fool idea I could get to the coast and find a way to get home. Then I had this accident – the rest you know.'

I was silent. Conrad had been trying to help a comrade. All any of them really wanted was to get back home. I knew exactly that feeling.

'I used to feel like that,' I said.

He turned and looked at me. 'But not any more?'

'No,' I said, and then added, 'I hated it to begin with. But now – now I think I love it better than anything. I would like to stay here always.'

'It is beautiful,' he agreed. He was silent for a while, then said, 'You and I, Choon, we are both victims of this war. This hateful war, started by a hateful man. I'm sorry about it, Choon.'

'It's not your fault,' I said, and suddenly I felt that whatever happened, I would do my utmost to see that Conrad came to no harm. I would protect him in any way I could. All of a sudden, in a musty dark hut with an enemy beside me, I was as brave as a lion.

I gathered up the bag and got to my feet. 'I'll leave the water bottle,' I said. 'I'll bring more. I'll work out a plan. Try to rest.'

The new moon came out from behind a cloud and in the dimness I saw a smile flit across his face. 'I can never thank you enough. But do not put yourself in danger, Choon. Go carefully.'

Chapter Twenty-two

I overslept next morning, a most unusual thing for me, not even stirring when Annie got up, and had to be awakened by Auntie Janet when she came to collect the week's school clothes for washing.

'June, are you all right? Annie says you had a bad headache last night. Is it better? By the way, your school blouse seems to be missing. Any idea where it is?'

I mumbled that I would look for it later. Auntie Janet paused, a bundle of laundry in her arms and peered down at me. 'You do look a bit peaky. Do you want to stay in bed for a bit?'

Still half-asleep, I thought quickly. I had to find some way of sneaking off to see Conrad, not easy when everyone was at home. I said, 'My head still aches a bit. I didn't sleep much. I'll get up soon.'

She reached out and laid a hand on my forehead. 'You're a bit warm. I hope you're not going down with something. Tell you what, Annie and Sylvia can do your Saturday jobs for you between them and you take it easy. I'll bring some breakfast up. What do you fancy?'

'I can get up, honest. But thank you,' I said hurriedly. I was getting to be a terrible liar and my conscience was beginning to trouble me. She gave me a pat and pulled the blankets up round my shoulders.

I lay there for a while feeling like a worm for telling lies to such a good, kind person as Auntie Janet, already rushed off her feet. What on earth would they all say if they knew? But then I thought of Conrad and forgot my scruples. I was in this up to my neck and I had to see it through, one way or another. I threw back the covers and got up.

It seemed very quiet, with everyone about their weekend tasks. If I was quick enough, I might be able to get some things together and go off while they were occupied. I made myself a cup of tea, boiled an egg and made some toast, speculating on how I could safely get more supplies to Conrad without detection. The boiled egg for a start. Conrad needed it more than I did. While Auntie Janet was out of the room, I found a paper bag and put in the egg, together with a couple of slices of toasted bread. Auntie Janet came in with some vegetables for dinner and I quickly stuffed the bag behind the sagging old kitchen sofa. Her sharp eyes at once noticed the breadcrumbs, the smell of toast and the egg saucepan.

'Oh, good, you've made yourself some breakfast. You must be feeling better.'

I wondered if the food I'd taken the night before had been missed. Nobody seemed to have noticed. When Auntie Janet went out again, I quickly found an empty lemonade bottle for water, a couple more rock cakes and a slice of cheese, which I added to the paper bag. I took it all upstairs. So far so good.

My idea of sneaking out this morning was doomed to failure, however. When I went downstairs again, Auntie Janet was still there, beginning preparations for dinner. 'I'm all behind this morning. June, if you're feeling better, would you give me a hand with the veg? Potatoes to peel and carrots to scrape. I've got to make some pastry for the rhubarb pie.'

I could not very well refuse, so stood at the sink peeling and scraping and wondering how I could get away alone later. Everyone came bursting in at dinnertime, noisy and hungry. Uncle Bill was in a grumpy mood again, grousing and complaining about a letter that had come, with notice that yet another of his fields was to be ploughed up for potatoes by order of the War Ag.

'This time I'll not take it,' he said. 'I've had about enough of them little Hitlers. Plough it up in the autumn, they say. They'll provide a new tractor if necessary, they say. Well, they can keep it! I need that four acres for next year's hay. I'm a stockman, this arable caper don't sit well with me. I need that bit of pasture for when I get my herd back. And my old Fordson is good enough for me!'

Auntie Janet looked worried, cutting a slice of rhubarb pie. 'But you have to do what they say, Bill. Everything's different now, and they have the power to evict us if we don't follow instructions. Don't forget that.'

'Evict us, my foot. This is my land, as it was my father's afore me, and I'll not budge, whatever they may say. And when they come to inspect that crop of spuds, I'll tell 'em.'

He pushed his plate to one side without touching the pie and stumped off, banging the back door.

'Oh dear, rhubarb's his favourite too,' said Auntie Janet, frowning. 'He takes this War Ag thing so hard. Sometimes he worries me.'

The anxious frown between her eyes seemed to deepen. I wished I could think of something to say that would make her feel better. But I could think of nothing but Conrad and the danger he was in, and my part in the dilemma. Without thinking, I said, 'Have they found that escaped POW yet?'

She began to clear the dishes. 'No, I don't think so. They seem to think he's got clear away from here somehow, and heading for the coast. But they'll catch him, never fear. Nothing for you to worry about.'

I felt like all kinds of a hypocrite. Sylvia was fussing about with her dress for the party, putting the flat irons to heat on the bars of the range. 'Annie and June, I'll do yours too while I'm at it.' She sighed. 'It's a pity we haven't got anything new to wear. They'll think we're poor as church mice, with only one dress each. Then I'm going to put my hair in curlers.'

'Perhaps you'd iron mine as well, while you're about it,' said Auntie Janet. 'It's in my wardrobe – the green one. I haven't worn it for ages.' She sighed again.

All of us looked at her in surprise. 'Does that mean you're going to the party as well?' asked Annie.

'Yes, it does. I got your dad to agree to go with me, and I'm going to hold him to it. It'll do him good to get out for a change and away from all this fretting and fuming.'

I thought Sylvia might not take kindly to this news, but she hardly turned a hair, and said, 'OK, I'll do that. Better iron Dad's best shirt as well.'

Auntie Janet turned to me. 'Are you feeling better, June? You've got more colour in your cheeks.'

'Yes, thank you, I am,' I said. 'The headache's gone.' And then, in a rush of desperation, I added, 'I think I'd like some fresh air, so is it OK if I go out for a bit?'

'Of course, love.' She smiled. 'You've really taken to the country now, haven't you? It's lovely to see. Some of the poor evacuee children don't like it at all.' She dumped a load of dishes in the stone sink.

'I'll help you with those first,' I added quickly, but she waved me away. 'No, no, Annie'll help. You go out and have a nice walk. Glad you're better. We'll all be able to go to the party together.'

She almost pushed me out of the door. That was Annie and Sylvia occupied, Tom was nowhere to be seen. I should be safe. I went upstairs and got my thick jumper, holding it bunched up with the bag of provisions inside.

'I don't think you'll need that today,' said Auntie Janet. 'The sun's out and it's quite warm.'

'I'm still feeling a bit shivery,' I lied, wondering again at the way the untruths rolled so glibly off my tongue.

'Well, don't stay out too long.'

'I won't.'

I had to be very careful of my movements, so set off through the orchard, across the cow pasture, where Marigold and Tulip were peacefully grazing, and into the coppice where bluebells stretched away under the beech trees. Any other day I'd have lingered there, watching the sun dappling the flowers, listening to the birdsong with the occasional call of a cuckoo. But today I was on a mission. I followed the stream bed until I was out of sight of the farm, and then doubled back and climbed the hedge into the Boggy Field.

Conrad was there in much the same place as before, and he looked scared and then relieved as I opened the door. 'Choon! I did not expect you yet.' He looked pale, with bluish shadows under his eyes as though he had not slept much. The foot looked swollen and he had not put the boot back on. A beam of sunshine with dust motes dancing in it stretched from the dirty window across the dusty straw.

I put down the provisions and said, 'They think I've been ill. I mustn't be long. Here's some more food, and water, and I got some bandages, proper ones, from the First Aid box, and a pair of Tom's socks. His feet are as big as yours now.'

'Ah, thank you. Just what I need. With my ankle bandaged and clean socks, I shall be all set to go on my way tonight.'

He was trying to sound light-hearted, but looking at the swollen purple ankle, I could not see him going anywhere.

'I won't be able to come tonight,' I said. 'There's a party we have to go to, at the American base, and we'll be late back. Sylvia and Annie will talk for hours and I won't be able to get away.'

'No,' he said. 'Don't come. You have done enough. I don't want to bring trouble to you. By tomorrow, I will be gone. Thank you, and goodbye. After the war, I will come back and thank you properly.'

I could see that he meant to go, whatever state he might be in. I felt a deep sadness, with fear mixed in. However could he get away? If he was caught, what then? The thought terrified me. I kept my head lowered as I rebandaged his ankle, so he would not see the tears in my eyes. 'Thank you,' he said. 'Don't stay any longer. Go back now. Goodbye and be happy.'

I gathered up the food remains, the paper bag, my torn-up blouse. I had a horrible, hollowed-out, sick feeling in my stomach, and the certainty that I would never see him again.

Chapter Twenty-three

I really did not want to go to the party, but there was nothing else for it. They would not leave me here alone if I said I did not want to go. There was a great bustle of activity as we got ready. Sylvia still mourned the fact that she had only the dress with the peplum that she could wear. But something else had cheered her up immensely. We had proper nylon stockings! Daisy and Milly had somehow obtained a whole pack of nylons and had passed on a pair each to Sylvia, Annie and me, and even some for Auntie Janet, although she said she could not wear them because her legs did not measure up any more. She also felt that Annie and I were a little young for such things, and that our white socks would be more suitable, but after a while she relented, with the provision that we must never let Uncle Bill know where the nylons had come from.

I smoothed the gossamer-like fabric, marvelling at its lightness and delicacy. You'd never know you had stockings on at all, except for the seam up the back. Sylvia warned us not to handle them too much or they would ladder.

She called me into her bedroom as we were getting ready, and offered to do my hair for me, as Daisy and Milly hadn't been able to come over this time. Sitting me in front of her little dressing-table mirror, she pulled my hair out of its usual plaits and spread it over my shoulders.

'You know, you have beautiful hair, June,' she said, beginning to brush it out, rather too vigorously for my liking. 'It's thick and shiny, and a lovely colour, sort of dark blonde. It's a waste to keep it in plaits. I'm going to leave it down for tonight.'

She worked busily, brushing my hair until it shone, and then pulling back a strand from each side and fastening it at the back, leaving the rest loose. The girl in the mirror looked quite different, almost a young lady.

'Thank you, Sylvia. I love it.'

She gave me a pat. 'You're going to be a beauty one day, you know that? When you've lost the puppy fat and grown a bit taller. You've got the cheekbones and the right bone structure.' She pulled a face, bending her head to look at her reflection beside mine in the mirror. 'Me, I'm pretty enough, but it's the chocolate-boxy kind. Still, plenty of actresses are like me. It's the acting ability that counts, not just the looks.'

'You really want to be an actress?'

'I really do. I know people think I just want to be famous and be a star and all that, but I really do want to act. I love drama at school.' She sighed. 'I'd love to go on to stage school, but not much chance, with a war on and everything. And Dad would be hopping mad if I even suggested it!'

'Oh, I hope you can!' I said. This was a different Sylvia, sharing her hopes and dreams, not the usual empty-headed girl she sometimes seemed. We are not all what we seem at first, I thought.

She sat back on the bed and hugged her knees. 'You know what? If that black chap asks me to dance again, I will, and I don't care what the rest say. If they try to fight, I'll report them. I think they treat those black soldiers dreadfully.'

I turned to look at her. I could see she really meant it, and I felt a wave of admiration. I didn't think I'd ever be as brave as that.

She jumped up. 'You'll do. We'd better get dressed. Is Annie getting ready?'

Annie had been lying on her bed when I last saw her, reading a book on animal diseases, since she had lately decided she was definitely going to be a vet. She had told me she thought animals were far more intelligent than humans. 'I'll go and see,' I said.

As I went, I suddenly realised that I had not thought about Conrad for almost an hour.

Despite it still being daylight outside, the party room at the American base was lit up like a fairground once you got inside. Auntie Janet whispered to me that it must have been the ballroom at Wayland Hall in the years before the war. It was decorated with brightly coloured bunting and strings of coloured lights. Long tables laden with food stretched down the middle; on a platform at the far end stood a microphone, musical instruments, drums. We gasped at the sight of the food, things we hadn't seen for a long time, sausage rolls, dainty sandwiches, pastries, iced cakes, jellies, all kinds of cheeses, little dishes of sweets and chocolates.

The room was full already, with a buzz of excited conversation. Uncle Bill had come with some reluctance, and he surveyed the scene with amazement. 'They know how to do theirselves well, the Yanks,' he muttered at sight of all the food.

'This is all for us, though,' said Auntie Janet quickly. 'I don't suppose they live like this every day.'

'Wouldn't be too sure of that,' he said. I could see he wasn't going to say a good word about the Americans, whatever happened. I was relieved that he had come, though. I'd had goose pimples thinking of what might have happened if he'd stayed home, decided to take a walk round the Boggy Field, gone into the hut…

We all, Uncle Bill included, did full justice to the refreshments when we sat down to them. GIs in uniform waited on us, replacing the emptied plates of food with full ones, refilling our lemonade glasses.

'Hi, there,' said a cheerful voice and there was Brad, looking very tall, holding a full jug with ice cubes clinking inside. 'How are you guys today? All looking very charming, if I may say so. And I hope you ladies are all ready to cut a rug afterwards?'

We said our hellos, and Sylvia quickly added, 'This is my mum and dad,' in case he should say something which might seem even more overfamiliar. Brad seemed equal to the occasion and reached over to shake them both by the hand. 'Very pleased to meet you, sir, and to see you again, ma'am.'

'Say what you like, they do have beautiful manners,' said Auntie Janet when he had moved on, and Uncle Bill for once did not disagree. A good meal always put him in a better mood, I'd noticed.

When we had eaten all we could, the tables were swiftly cleared and taken down for the dancing. On the stage, a group of musicians were tuning up their instruments. When they struck up a lively dance tune, people were soon on the floor, girls in bright dresses, men in white shirts, Americans in their smart uniforms. I remembered the fight last time and looked around for the black soldiers. As before, they seemed to be in a group by themselves, near the door. I wondered whatever would happen if Sylvia kept her promise and danced with one of them. But there were plenty of others to partner her. Auntie Janet and Uncle Bill sat with other parents, talking between themselves as best they could above the music.

I was surprised to see that Uncle Bill seemed more relaxed, even tapping his foot in time to the music, and that Auntie Janet seemed quite animated and younger somehow, in a green-flowered dress I hadn't seen before. Before long, some of the older couples began to take to the floor, and to my astonishment, Uncle Bill and Auntie Janet were among them. I realised that they must have been young themselves once, young and carefree and full of hope, before they'd been overtaken by the cares and toil and disappointments of work and war.

'Care to dance, ma'am?' said a voice in my ear, and Brad was there again, holding out his hand. I thought he must mean Sylvia, and looked over my shoulder, but she was already dancing with someone else. Tom and Annie had disappeared in groups of their friends from school. It was me he meant.

I felt my cheeks growing pink. 'I – I'm not very good.'

'Don't worry, I'll teach you,' he said. 'Just follow my lead.'

And suddenly there I was, floating around the floor with the best-looking soldier there, in my opinion. He was a good dancer and I had no problem in following his lead and picking up the steps. It wasn't long before I found that I was enjoying myself.

'You look very pretty this evening, June,' he said. When he smiled, I noticed that his teeth were beautifully white. 'You've done your hair a different way. Suits you.'

I'd had my first grown-up compliment and I didn't know what to say.

'Sylvia did it,' I murmured, and found myself babbling on, 'She's very clever with hair, and she's a really nice person...'

He smiled again. 'Never doubted it. You Brits are all swell, or the ones I've met anyway. But you're a little different, not quite as shy as the rest of your family, I've noticed. Why's that, I wonder?'

I thought, here we go again, having to explain myself. 'Maybe because they're not my family. I'm an evacuee, from London.'

'Ah. Now that would explain it.'

I remembered that Conrad had said much the same thing, and my heart gave a sudden lurch. Conrad! I'd forgotten him again!

The dance finished and we sat down. I thought Brad would wander off to dance with someone else, maybe

Sylvia, but he sat down beside me, just as though I was a grown-up person, and asked if I would like a drink, and fetched me lemonade with ice clinking in the glass. He had one too, and touched my glass and said, 'Cheers!' before we drank.

'Tell me about yourself,' he said.

I couldn't see what there was to tell, but once I'd started I found there was lots. So I told him about home, and Mum, and Dad in the army, and the bombing, and Boots, and how I'd hated it here when I first came. I even told him about the War Ag and how much Uncle Bill detested them, but I didn't mention prisoners of war. When I paused for breath, he gave a low whistle.

'Wow! You've been through some stuff for a kid your age. Kids back home wouldn't believe it.'

I felt myself deflate like a burst balloon. That was what I was to him, just a kid. He might have danced with me and talked like he would to an adult, but that was how he saw me. Not thirteen until September, and he must be all of eighteen. I was surprised at myself. I hadn't thought I liked him that much. I put down my glass and got to my feet. 'I think Auntie Janet is looking for me,' I said.

He looked surprised too. 'Oh, OK. Say, it's been real nice chatting to you, though.'

Yes, it had been nice, and more than nice. I didn't know anything about falling in love, except what I'd read in Sylvia's magazines, but maybe it felt a bit like this, kind of exciting but comfortable as well. But I needn't fool myself, because he regarded me as no more than a child.

Auntie Janet was at the other side of the room, sitting down with the rest of the older people, fanning herself with a paper napkin after the dancing. On the way over to her, I bumped into Tom, mooching along through the crowd with his hands in his pockets. 'I don't suppose you're going to dance any more now,' he said grumpily.

'I don't know,' I said. 'I might. What's the matter?'

'I suppose you'll only dance with that Yank,' he said, staring down at his shoes.

I didn't answer for a moment, then I realised that Tom was being grumpy because he was jealous. He wanted me to dance with him. I'd danced with him last time and this time I hadn't. Well, I thought, too bad, I don't feel like dealing with a moody fourteen-year-old just now. But I just said, 'I don't think I want to dance any more. I'm tired now. I really hope we go home soon.'

Chapter Twenty-four

In spite of the late night, I was up very early the next morning. Nobody else was about, not even Uncle Bill. I sneaked off on my devious route through the meadow, the woodland and back to the hut in the potato field. I don't know what I expected to find, but I had this rather forlorn hope that by now Conrad had gone, and had somehow miraculously reached a place where he could find his way home.

In that I was disappointed. He was still there, curled up on the straw, and turned a flushed, sweating face to me as I went in. His ankle was still swollen and discoloured, and I could see a couple of angry red streaks stretching up the leg. He said in a croaky voice, 'Choon, I'm sorry, I think I have fever. Have you brought water?'

I had, along with some cold bacon and bread I'd taken from the dairy. I gave him a drink, helping him to sit up and holding the glass bottle because he seemed so shaky. He waved away the food.

'Choon, I am thinking, I have to give myself up. I am sick. I was a fool to do what I did.' He paused. 'Choon, I want you to go back to the farm and say you have seen something suspicious while you were out for a walk.

Then they'll come and find me. Don't say you helped me, and I'll say nothing about you. Will you do that?'

'No,' I said. 'I won't.' A cold fear was clutching at my insides. 'You'll be punished, you might be shot…' I couldn't go on.

'I don't think so,' he said. 'You British are known for fair treatment. They won't shoot a sick man. I will be all right. I would rather go back and take what's coming than die here like a rabbit in a trap.'

'You won't die,' I said. 'And I *won't* give you up.' I could hear the desperation in my own voice.

'Then what *will* you do?'

I had no answer. I could not look after a sick man on my own, in secret. I had no way of getting medicines. Desperate ideas floated through my mind. I could ask someone for help. Someone I could trust. But who?

Would Auntie Janet think of helping? I wondered. She'd liked Conrad. But she'd never go against her husband, and he would certainly not be a party to concealing an escaped prisoner of war. Annie? No, she was even younger than me, I couldn't involve her. Sylvia? She seemed the likeliest. She'd shown she cared about those who were unfairly treated. She'd liked Conrad too. And she loved a bit of drama. I was still considering this possibility when another voice made me suddenly freeze.

'June! June! Are you there?'

A boy's voice, newly broken but still inclined to squeak embarrassingly at times. Tom!

He was getting closer. He mustn't be allowed to come in here.

'Quick!' I told Conrad. 'Get under the straw!'

155

He shuffled position and I piled more straw over him. Then I quickly left the hut and closed the door behind me. When I sauntered round the hut to the other side, trying to pretend I was out for a casual morning stroll, I saw Tom coming around the grass headland that bordered the field. I went to meet him, trying to put as much distance as I could between us and the hut with its occupant. He was frowning slightly.

'June, what are you doing?'

'Nothing,' I said quickly – too quickly, for he looked at me suspiciously. 'I'm just out for a walk. I like walking. I like looking at nature and stuff.' My voice sounded unnaturally high and breathless.

He was not convinced, narrowing his eyes and squinting at me.

'You're up to something. I can tell. You can't fool me.'

'Don't be silly.'

'You've got something in the hut. You've been taking food and water. What is it, a fox or something? The farmers shoot foxes, it would be just like you to hide one and take care of it.'

This was so near the truth and yet so far that I almost felt like giggling hysterically. I'd had no idea that Tom had noticed I'd been taking food and water. He was peering hard at me, frowning, not budging. 'I'm going to find out. I'm going to look. Whatever you're doing, I came to warn you – Dad and the War Ag man are coming to look at the spuds today, and Dad's in a mood. You're a dope, but I didn't want you to get in trouble with whatever you're doing, you and Annie.'

'It's nothing to do with Annie,' I said quickly.

He pounced upon that. 'Oh, so there *is* something! I knew it! Come on, I'm going to find out what.'

He looked so smug I could have walloped him.

All in a moment, I had to decide. I could go on trying to fob Tom off, which looked like being a losing battle, or I could tell him the truth, and trust him to do the right thing. I made the decision.

'Look,' I said. 'It's not a fox. It's a man. It's Conrad. He's the one who escaped, and he's hurt and sick, and I've been trying to help him. Only now I don't know what to do…'

I felt my voice wobble and tears come to my eyes. I blinked them back furiously. Tom whistled, a long slow sound through his teeth. 'So that's it. Well, I'm blowed! Let's go and see.'

Conrad was still buried in the straw, but I could see his boot and part of his shoulder. 'Conrad, Tom's here. I'm sorry, I wasn't careful enough.'

Conrad's face came out, white now but still sweating, and he struggled to sit up, but sank back with a groan. 'Tom. Have you told your father?'

Tom squatted down beside him. 'No, I only just found out. Listen, Conrad, I'm going to help you. Don't know how, but we'll work something out. Only I don't think you should stay here. There's going to be people all over the field today. It's not safe.'

It would be unkind to say that he was relishing the situation, but I could see he was quite taking to the idea of an adventure, something that might happen in one of his comics. He sat back on his heels. 'Let me think.' He was quiet for a moment, then suddenly groaned and put his head in his hands. 'Oh no! I forgot – I was coming to tell June about the War Ag, but there's something else. We heard on the wireless that they've decided you haven't got to the coast after all, but might have stayed around here. They're going to search all the farms again, and the woods and fields and everywhere. They're using dogs…'

Conrad sank back on the straw and groaned, looking whiter than before, if that was possible. 'Then I'm done for. You must take Choon and get yourselves away, don't tell anyone you've been involved in any way. I'll surrender when they come…'

I could feel the blood draining from my own face and panic rising in my stomach. It was all happening too fast. And then as though in echo to my thoughts, I heard a new sound that set my heart thumping as though it would burst from my chest. The sound of dogs, more than one, still faint and far away, but barking and baying as hounds do when they are on the trail of a fox.

Chapter Twenty-five

I'd seen fox hunting once or twice, since I'd been living on the farm. Auntie Janet told me there used to be hunting almost every weekend before the war came. The hunt had been obliged to cut right back as part of the war effort. Annie was dead against fox hunting, said it was a cruel sport and when she was older she would set up a campaign against it. I was inclined to agree when she told me what happened, how a fox was torn to pieces when the hounds got it, and that young children were 'blooded' when a fox was caught, its tail cut off and its blood smeared on the face of the child. It made me feel sick when she told me. But all the same, there was something rather spectacular about seeing a hunt in full cry, the men in red coats on sleek, well-groomed horses, the rallying call of the hunter's horn, the mass of beautiful, baying, running, brown-and-white foxhounds hot on the trail. But my sympathies were still all with the fox.

I felt myself freeze. 'They may not be coming here,' I said, clutching at straws. 'It may just be the hunt.'

Tom shook his head. 'It's them. There's been some rain over the last few days but not enough to wash out the trail. We've got to get Conrad out of here.'

I looked at Conrad, ashen-faced on the straw. 'How can we?'

'Let me think. If we could get something, a wheelbarrow, or a cart, we might be able to move him…'

I felt on the verge of hysterical laughter again at the thought of pushing an escaped POW in a wheelbarrow. Where would we go? How far could we hope to get? But I had no other idea.

'Go home!' gasped Conrad. 'Go on, now!'

Neither of us budged. I had a surge of thankfulness that I was not facing this alone, that Tom was there, with his mouth set in a stern line and his beautiful eyes darkened with this dilemma.

And then we heard voices – raised, angry voices.

Tom frowned and looked out of the grimy little window. 'It's Dad. And the War Ag man. They're here, in this field, they'll be walking all over it. Looks like trouble.'

As if we hadn't enough already, I thought. I joined him at the window. Uncle Bill and the man were standing at the far end of the ridged rows of growing potatoes, waving their arms and talking loudly. Uncle Bill was almost bellowing, his voice carrying clear across the field. 'I'll not plough another inch, I'm telling you! And you can threaten to evict me all you like! This farm is mine and here I'll stay. You'll have to carry me out!'

I could not tell what the other man said but he sounded angry too. They began to walk between the rows, coming our way, the War Ag man poking at the growing potatoes with his stick every so often. Then another movement caught my eye in the opposite corner of the field. A dog, a big dog, was sniffing about the hedgerows and around the dry ditch where I'd first found Conrad hidden. As I watched, transfixed with horror, a man appeared, climbing the hedge with a great splintering and snapping of branches and twigs, catching the dog and fastening a leash on its collar, scolding it for escaping. He was joined by another man and another dog on a leash.

Uncle Bill had seen them too. I heard him roar across at them, 'Get off my land! What do you think you're doing, breaking down my hedges? Get off my land!'

One of the men shouted back something I couldn't hear, and Uncle Bill roared back, 'There's no ruddy escaped prisoner here! You're messing up my crops! I'm going to ruddy report you!'

I grabbed at Tom's hand in terror. 'What shall we do, oh, what shall we do?' He had no answer, but kept hold of my hand and it was strangely comforting. I prayed, silently, 'God, keep Conrad safe! Oh, keep him safe!'

Behind us, I could hear Conrad's harsh breathing as he tried to struggle to his feet. The men and dogs were still coming, down the ridges of potatoes, carelessly trampling the neatly weeded rows. I heard the War Ag man say, 'That's government property you're destroying!'

But still they came, the dogs' eager noses questing about, into the ditch and out again, eager for fresh scents.

'We have to go out there,' said Tom. 'Maybe we can distract them.'

It was a vain hope but there seemed nothing else to do. We opened the door, closing it behind us, and faced the two groups, coming closer together as they moved down the field. Everyone, especially Uncle Bill and the War Ag man, seemed angry, and Uncle Bill was even angrier when he saw the two of us. 'What the heck are you two doing here? Go on home, this is no place for children, ruddy world gone mad!'

The two military men came on, sharp eyes taking in every detail. The two lots of men met very close to the hut. 'Mr Powell?' said the one who seemed to be in charge. 'We are authorised to search your land and premises for the prisoner of war who escaped. We have reason to believe he came this way. Have you seen anything suspicious at all?'

'No, I haven't, and I'm authorised to tell you that you are trespassing on my land, breaking down my hedges and trampling on my crops. And you are terrorising my children!' He turned to us, face red and furious. 'Tom, June, get back to the house this instant. Go on, move! Don't stand there like goobies!'

I couldn't have moved if I'd wanted to. My legs were trembling violently. I reached for Tom's hand again and held on to it tight. 'Dad…' he began, and then I screamed, because I saw that the dogs were now sniffing around the door of the hut.

Uncle Bill turned on his son. 'Tom, I told you, take her home. She's terrified of those there dogs.'

The dogs were sniffing around the walls and door of the hut, nosing about in the long grass. One of the men was peering in through the grimy window. I prayed that Conrad had burrowed deep into the straw.

The War Ag man was watching all this, a nasty sneering expression on his thin face. 'I see you manage your children about as well as you manage your farm, Powell,' he said. 'And a fat lot of notice they take! About what I'd expect from an awkward cuss like you.'

And then things happened faster than I could blink. Out of the corner of my eye, I saw a movement in the doorway of the hut. And then the dogs were there, let off their leashes and growling deep in their throats. I gripped Tom's hand, feeling waves of dizziness and a swirling blackness in front of my eyes. The dogs were in the hut, I could hear a horrible snarling and one sharp cry, and shouts from the men. I remembered Annie's description of a fox torn to pieces by the hounds. And then the darkness rose and seemed to swallow me up.

Chapter Twenty-six
Juniper

Nana's face grew very sad as she related, and relived, this terrible event. She looked tired, and very old all of a sudden. For a while she was silent, twisting her hands in her lap, as though she had forgotten I was there, forgotten everything except that terrible day.

I said, tentatively, 'Nana, are you OK?'

She seemed to return to the present day with a start. She looked at the clock on the wall by the patio door. 'Oh, Juni. We've talked so long. I do believe it's almost time for you to go.'

Today was Friday, and it was the last afternoon of our time together. Tomorrow Dad, Mom and I were off on our big adventure. I'd been looking forward to it since Dad told me, but now, suddenly, I felt torn. A big part of me wanted to continue with Nana, to listen to her soft British voice with just the hint of an American inflection, telling of a time in her past that had stayed alive in her mind in a way that was clearer to her perhaps than the events of the week before. I'd fetched her drinks and ice cream, we'd taken little walks together on the shady side of the street, we'd napped indoors in the cool in the afternoons, woken refreshed and carried on with her story. But I didn't want it to end there, with that tragic scene.

I thought, maybe by the time I get back, Nana's condition will have changed, maybe her memory will have faded. I said, 'There's still half an hour. There's lots I want to know still.'

She took a long drink from the glass beside her and said, 'Well, fire away.'

I didn't quite know where to start. But one thing had been bothering me for some time now. I realised with shame that I didn't know who my great-grandfather had been, who Nana had married, how she had landed up in America and set up the organisation called Reconcile, although I was beginning to think I could guess. I wouldn't know until I asked, so I came right out with it. 'Nana, did you marry Brad?'

She looked surprised for a moment, then laughed. 'Oh no, I didn't marry Brad. Sylvia did.'

That was a surprise, but it didn't answer my question. I thought, so, it must have been Tom. Tom with the beautiful eyes, who wanted to dance with her and who had done his best to help her save Conrad.

'It was Tom, then,' I said.

She laughed again. 'Wrong again! No, it wasn't Tom either. Haven't your parents taught you anything about your family history?'

They hadn't, actually. They were always far too busy to sit talking to me about anything except the things that directly concerned me here and now. I resolved that I would make a point of insisting we sat and talked on this coming vacation. Maybe we could sit out under the stars, even round a campfire, if we were in a place where we were allowed to make a fire. I felt a stirring of excitement.

Nana's eyes had grown dreamy again. 'No, it wasn't Tom either, Juni. I married Conrad.'

That made me sit up straight again, almost spilling my own drink. 'Conrad! But – but he was killed! The dogs – ' I shuddered, not even able to face thinking about it.

'No.' Suddenly the weariness seemed to fall away from Nana and she looked young again. I could see the beauty that she must have been as a young woman, as Sylvia had predicted she would be. 'He didn't die; those dogs were not trained to kill. They took him away and patched him up, treated the infection and set the broken bones. He made a full recovery, except that he had a slight limp all his life because the ankle hadn't been properly treated to begin with. He returned to Germany after the war, and came back to see us all a few years later.' Her eyes were soft, remembering. 'He was a lovely man, your great-grandfather. A lovely, lovely man. We became great friends with Brad and Sylvia, and it was through them we came to live in the United States, where there were greater opportunities than in post-war Europe.' She chuckled. 'And he called me Choon to the end of his days.'

I pondered all of this for a moment. 'So I am a little bit German,' I said.

'You are one-eighth German. One-eighth British. And lots of other things as well. Your gramps, my son-in-law, is half Native American. Your mother is a quarter Spanish. You have the blood of many fine races in your veins, Juni. You should be proud.'

My head was spinning. I knew about Gramps, and Mom, but this new information sent my mind into overdrive, thinking of what percentage of each race I had.

'You are a citizen of the world, Juni,' said Nana gently, as though she could read my mind. 'And please God, one day you'll be a citizen of Heaven. While you're in the world, walk tall. You are unique, created and loved by God to be the very best you can be.'

I felt proud and humbled all at once. Whatever ancestry I had, I was me, I was loved and I was valued. I would do my best. I felt a big lump rise in my throat.

But there were still questions I wanted to ask. The people Nana had known as a girl had become very real to me. There was still a little time left before I had to go.

'Nana,' I said. 'Tell me what happened to the others. Did Sylvia get to be a famous actress?'

She smiled. 'No. But her daughter did, all the way to Hollywood. Sylvia and Brad were so proud of her. You've probably heard of her, or seen her films. Diana Devine was her stage name.'

Another big surprise. Diana Devine, or DeeDee as she was known, was one of my very favourite movie stars. So that was the connection! She must be an old lady herself now, but she had been so beautiful and talented.

'Wow,' I said. 'And how about Annie and Tom?'

'Annie became a vet, and later a pioneer in animal medicines. She never married. She always said that animals were more intelligent than humans. Maybe she was right. And Tom, dear Tom. He farmed with his father, though he was far more even-tempered, married a farmer's daughter, raised a family. I visited them all whenever I went home to the UK. They became my family, you know. I never went back to London to live. My dad was killed in action shortly after that spring, and my mother died just months later. I believe she died of a broken heart. Uncle Bill and Auntie Janet kept me and brought me up as their own.'

She was looking sad again. I hated to leave her like that. She went on, 'They're all dead now, of course. I have no one left who remembers those times. No one at all.'

'But you have us,' I said, wishing I could think of something more cheering and comforting to say.

'Yes, I have you. And you must go soon and get ready for your big adventure.'

Luciana had arrived and I could hear her clattering pans in the kitchen. Then the doorbell buzzed and she went to answer it.

'Mrs June,' she said, sliding open the patio door. 'There's someone at the door who'd like to see you. A gentleman.'

'Whoever can that be? Ask him to come out here, please, Luciana.'

Luciana was soon back and following her was a tall, bronzed man with neatly trimmed thick white hair. He came across at once and took Nana's hand. 'June? It's really you? Do you remember me?'

His accent wasn't quite British and not quite American, something in between. I guessed it was what they call mid-Atlantic.

Nana had that little line between her eyes that meant she was thinking hard. 'I don't believe I do. But please pull up a chair and sit down. Can we offer you a cool drink? It's hot again this afternoon.'

A pair of blue eyes twinkled at her. He took a seat, crossing his long legs and smiling, a person very much at ease in any surroundings. He didn't give his name, but said teasingly, 'I'd have known you anywhere, but we do go back a very long way. We spent a day together once, a very long day, remember?'

And suddenly a light seemed to dawn in Nana's eyes. 'Freddie? Surely it can't be – little Freddie?'

He stood and made a little bow. 'It can, and it is! Frederick J Cotterill at your service!' He paused, becoming serious. 'I never forgot you, June. You took such good care of me that day.'

Nana was leaning forward, suddenly animated. 'But what happened? You never came to our school. You just seemed to disappear.'

He sat down again and laughed, a deep rumbling laugh. 'My parents – my adoptive parents – moved almost right away after that. My dad had a condition that prevented him going into the services, but they were a wealthy family and he was a successful man too. I went to the best schools, lived in a big house, went to university. We travelled. I had a great life, a fantastic privileged life. I went into the family business and we moved to the US forty years ago. I'm retired now, my wife died three years ago and I've been a bit lonely since then, doing quite a lot of travelling. I live not so far away from here now. Did some detective work and found where you were. I've always remembered you, and so much wanted to thank you for taking care of me that day.'

I looked at his Rolex watch, his Gucci shoes, expensive casual shorts and shirt, and thought of the poverty-stricken, spindly legged, undernourished little boy Nana had taken under her wing that day. She didn't seem to be noticing any of those things, but was leaning forward eagerly and looking into his tanned face with the deep laughter lines around the eyes and mouth. 'Oh, Freddie, how wonderful! You must tell me all the details – everything!'

'And you must tell me all about your life. Is this young lady your granddaughter?'

'Great-granddaughter,' said Nana. 'She's a treasure.'

I was rather embarrassed by this and it was a relief when my phone buzzed.

'Juniper,' Mom sounded on the verge of being cross. 'It's already 5.30. You need to be home to finish your packing. Dad and I will come round to say goodbye to Nana later. She's going to miss you, but I'm sure she'll be OK.'

This had been my big worry, that Nana would not be OK, that over the three weeks she would deteriorate, she would forget, and that when we came back she would be a changed person. Now, looking across at her and Freddie, his white head and her shady pink hat close together, already deep in animated reminiscence of the past, I knew that my worries were groundless. Already I could sense the rapport between them. Together they would share, and remember, the hard times and the good, the highs and the lows. And I would take home my notebook and I would record my Nana's story, so that whatever happened she would never be forgotten.

'Sorry, Mom,' I said. 'I just forgot the time. Nana is fine, she has a visitor. I'll be home in five.'

Historical Note

Chapter Nineteen

In 1940, a farmer from Wiltshire who refused to leave his farm was shot by a member of the Wartime Agricultural Committee. He died of his wounds.

See article by Brian Short in the *Agricultural History Review* entitled: 'Death of a Farmer: The Fortunes of War and the Strange Case of Ray Walden'.

www.jstor.org/stable/40276268